THE DRUID
OF SKELLS

Anthea Jackson

Pixel  tweaks
PUBLICATIONS

Published in 2016
© Copyright Anthea Jackson

Second print run copy

ISBN: 978-0-9934679-6-7

Book interior & Cover Design by Russell Holden
www.pixeltweakspublications.com

Pixel❈tweaks
PUBLICATIONS

THE DRUID OF SKELLS

Prologue

Miles Hardisty, riding homeward from his errand at the Big House, suddenly drew rein. What a strangely-twisted dead tree that was, outlined against the fading orange horizon. He turned the horse for a better look. Yes – it was no tree but a tall gaunt figure against the skyline, a loose robe flapping against it in the sharp wind. It stood quite still, fists raised as if in threat, while twilight thickened behind it. After a while, Miles could no longer make it out with any certainty. He rode on, quickly. He would take good care not to be caught by twilight at Skells again.

Contents

Tuesday October 12th

Letter from Miss Araminta Lewthwaite to her sister Louisa of High Stott Hall, Low Furness

My Dearest Louisa,

I take up my pen at the earliest opportunity to reassure my beloved family of my safe arrival at Skells. It is a strangely romantic and magnificent spot, hallowed by sacred ruins ivy mantled and owl haunted. How would I not delight in your company, dear Louisa, as we together explore its beauties! I shall convey them to you as I am able to observe them more closely, for it was darkening when we arrived, and the swaying lights on the trim vehicle Lord Fenborough sent to Ripley for us showed nothing beyond glimpses of tree trunks.

Three days it is since, with indescribable emotions, I parted from all who are dearest to me. Long as I had desired to visit my old school friend and relive our happy days at Mrs Martindale's academy in York, my heart failed within me, as I wondered if I should ever again behold my beloved ones and the dear chimneys of my childhood home. As we passed through our gateway I envied Celestine her composure; she, less sensible of the parting moment, was occupied in ascertaining that all our luggage was duly stowed.

Despite my melancholy imaginings, after a while I began to enjoy the ride through the sunny lanes, still firm from the early frost, even though we had to move slowly lest we left the luggage cart too far behind

All was peaceful until we came to cross the sands. You may recall, Louisa, that but a year ago the treacherous tide snatched away a young gentleman and his horse as they neared Arnside; and within the memory of many have whole equipages been stuck fast in the quicksands, with the appalled would-be rescuers powerless to do aught but witness the frenzied plunging of the horses and the dying moans of the poor wretches incarcerated within as the racing tide doomed them to oblivion! Small wonder that I trembled as our mounts left the high road. The breeze freshened and the rivulets between the sandbars shivered and seemed, to my timorous gaze, to become wider and deeper as we approached. The first splash of the horses' hooves caused a tremor to run through me, and the poor dumb beasts themselves were hesitant and needed our encouraging voices. At one moment the wheels of the cart carrying our luggage became clogged in a patch of soft sand. I was in deadly fear for my new muslin but John and Peter, seemingly as calm as if they had to do this every day, jumped down up to their knees in the swirling stream and pushed at the wheels until, with a horrid sound as of a greedy giant balked of his prey, the sand released them. With what anxiety we then followed the road marked out by the guide posts, hoping that no sinister vagary of wind or tide had rendered them useless, or, worse, a snare.

With what exquisite relief we reached the firm ground of

Arnside, and repaired to the inn for refreshment and to rest the horses! I was somewhat vexed that a deal of sticky mud had splashed up to the skirts of my new habit, but consoled myself with the thought that Celestine would take but five minutes to remove the stain, and that adventures must have their attendant costs. And indeed, how often in the stories we love has not a 'travel stained wayfarer' gratefully accomplished his perilous journey.

And how welcome did Marianne and Edgar make us at their home in Lancaster! Little Araminta is the finest baby ever, and I warrant she will be a great beauty - far more so that the aunt whose namesake she is. (Does not 'aunt' carry with it a forbidding sound?)

Upon the next day we said farewell to our horses which were to stay for a while in Edgar's stables and watched John and Peter set off home with the cart. It would have been a melancholy moment but for the bustle of our own departure. Edgar placed us in the stagecoach (and what an excitement to be riding through the countryside with a group of total strangers. I hope I was in good looks, and did not show how unaccustomed I was to the experience. There was a fine looking young man in a blue coat opposite to me, but he spent the whole stage intent upon the book he was reading.)

We made our way to Kirby Lonsdale, sparing a few minutes after we had changed horses to gaze upon the River Lune flowing swiftly through its gorge; then, on over the bleak moorlands to Skipton There is a towering hill behind the village of Ingleton, fine enough to draw gasps of admiration from those who know not the rugged mountains of our native heath. The next day took us across more wildernesses, though as we came down towards Ripon and its massy cathedral the landskip became much flatter and more cultivated.. Many, nay most, would no doubt prefer the appearance of pastoral prosperity to wild heathland, but not the truly sensible soul which lodges in such bosoms as thine and mine! At Ripley we alighted from the coach and were by met by Lord Fenborough's coachman who had brought his lordship's vehicle. Then, at nightfall, we arrived.

The rattling coach stopped, and I was suddenly awoken by the voices of coachman and the lodge keeper. I peered out at the gateway reaching high above us. As the keeper opened the gates I saw dimly the huge shapes of twin dragons with outspread wings atop the gateposts, as it were guarding the entry. In the light of the flickering torch they leapt into life, seeming to turn their heads to stare at us with lofty disdain as we passed between them and entered their domain.

There was a long drive up to the house, and I must own that my heart failed me for a moment as I passed through the elegant doorway into a large and lofty hall, blazing with many candles. Celestine took my arm to help me across the threshold and I entered upon the unaccustomed magnificence I held up my chin and reminded myself firmly that Papa is just as truly a gentleman as Laetitia's noble father.

Dear Laetitia and her parents welcomed me with great

kindness, and after supper I retired to my chamber, where I have been sitting writing to you before a great fire. I have not yet met her brother Frederick, but I hear he is mighty handsome and a great horseman. He is almost twenty one, four years older than his sister, as she and I were born within a month of one another.

Write to me as often as you can; I shall write by every post

Your own
Araminta

* * *

While this letter was writing in Araminta's room, two young housemaids, Betty and Sarah were talking in the small attic they shared. Sarah was eager to learn about the new arrival. "Have you seen her yet? What does she look like?"

"I had a good look at her, yes, when I took the hot water in. She's busy writing a letter. She seems to be pretty enough with a pleasing voice."

"Nothing else, Betty?"

"I don't think as how she has all that much sense, sitting up scribbling away, after being in a coach for two days and a good warm bed waiting for her."

"Perhaps she's writing to a beau!"

"I don't reckon so. Why do you think she chooses to come just now?"

"To see the young mistress as she was at school with."

"The young mistress has been back home above a twelve month. Why did she never come afore? I don't think it's the young mistress but the young master she's come to see."

"But Betty, why should you think such a thing? Surely 'tis not the way a young lady would …"

"There may be no harm meant. But I'd say she's no chance of catching him. She's not that good looking but that he'd want a deal more brass than I reckon she's got from what I've seen of her gear. Her maid was setting out her clothes and none of them wasn't a patch on Miss Laetitia's"

"But if she really is a pleasant young lady, surely she wouldn't …"

"Oh Sarah, Sarah, the gentry can't be nice in choosing partners. You and me now if we were to like a young man as likes us and has enough to wed on, that's one thing but the ladies, poor things, has to set out their looks to catch some young man rich enough to live on in comfort. They can't look after themselves like we can. Now give over and stop pestering me, it's high time we were asleep with all we have to see to the morrow. Good night."

" Betty, before you blow out the candle… have you heard ought amiss … tonight?"

I have not, because there's nothing to hear, only silly nonsense made up to frighten us. If you're afraid say your prayers and keep your head under the clothes."

Betty extinguished the candle, and in that room at least all was quiet.

Wednesday October 13th

Araminta was awake when the maid drew the heavy curtains and let in the bright sunlight. Eager to see what she could she crossed to the window and, shivering despite her wrap and the cheerful fire, gazed out into the park. All was fresh looking in the early sun, each grass blade and brown leaf edged with a neat rim of hoar-frost. There were shreds of mist in the hollows, gently dispersing as the sun rose. In the distance under a clump of trees something moved, a grey brown shadow, then another, and another. Gradually they resolved themselves into creatures, one large with a branching head and nine or ten smaller. They were bigger than the dappled deer she sometimes glimpsed in the wood at home, but deer they must be. She watched them, secure at a distance, feeding among the trees. Suddenly a black and white spaniel ran through the grass towards them; the deer looked up and went, without panic or apparent haste. She watched them merge into the thinning mist, then turned to the room and her preparations for the day.

After breakfast she and Laetitia had their first opportunity for free conversation. It was some time before they recovered the ease there had been between them at school, for they had not seen each other since the day they left Mrs Martindale's academy, exchanging embraces, embroidered purses, and vows of eternal friendship. Fifteen months in the enclosure of family and family friends had bred some strangeness; Laetitia felt her friend a little remote from her world, perhaps even a little unpolished while Araminta ,replying to polite queries about her family, and listening to Laetitia's accounts of her new gowns and visits in the neighbourhood, felt with a touch of dismay that she seemed as placid and circumscribed as the deer in her father's park. Perhaps she herself would be the little spaniel to disturb the peace. She leant down and fondled the little white dog Laetitia had put on the sofa between them. It leapt to its feet, lashing its feathery tail and barking defiance. Both girls laughed and Araminta asked, " Do you remember Mrs Martindale's little dog.? Nobody could enter the dining room without his rousing the whole house. Such a tiny creature too."

"That night when he woke us all up! We all hid under the clothes believing thieves were breaking in-"

"Or that Jane Erskine was eloping after all! You recall how she told us younger ones such stories about the handsome young officer against whom her parents were so unjustly prejudiced, and how he would come one night in a coach and whisk her off to Gretna. Did she ever show you the strand of hair she wore in her locket?"

"Yes, it was a rather common ginger colour, I think, though we all agreed to call it a most romantic Titian shade."

"Did you ever believe her, Laetitia? I know I did when I was fourteen. I have heard from Catherine- you remember little Catherine who cried for a week when her white kitten died? – that she is now one of the teachers and taking drawing classes and giving lessons on the harp? Poor thing! I don't begrudge her her handsome young officer one bit, even if she was making game of us."

"You remember Sophie, who always swore she would marry no man but a brigand chief? She's engaged now, to her father's curate. She writes that he is handsome and tall with curly whiskers which I do not think is at all suitable for a clergyman. Our rector is grey haired and corpulent: my mother says he is a worthy man, certainly his sermons are dull enough."

"Dear Sophie! Do you remember the day when the three of us asked permission to buy some cherry ribbons for your new bonnet? What a time we had afterwards persuading Mrs Martindale that it took three and a half hours to find the right shade."

"And all the time we were strolling round the walls amusing ourselves with looking at all the people."

"You mean the officers! The 96th had just come to town and all the young officers were taking the air along the walls that morning. You must recall it."

"For shame, Araminta!"

"And we had to spend the whole evening removing your pretty blue ribbons and putting on the far less becoming cherry ones…. come, Laetitia, do not look so distressed. All our childish adventures are locked within my heart to any but you."

"O throw away the key. We are now grown women."

Araminta was quick to change the subject, severally painful as it was to each. "I sometimes wonder what I gained from my time at school, apart from your friendship. It is true I can recite the rivers of Yorkshire, the Kings and Queens of England and the order of the planets-"

"But you never could manage the Kings of Israel and Judah. I used to try and help you but they are not good names to whisper."

"No indeed! Rehoboam, Jeroboam, Hezekiah! How much more sensible we are to stick to Edwards and Henrys in the main. But I liked some history, like the poor little princes in the tower and their wicked murdering uncle."

My brother says no Yorkshireman believes he killed them, but I wonder if that can be right. He is a most horrid man in the picture beside the story."

"I remember, he was a hunchback and born with all his teeth too! And Mary Queen of Scots, so beautiful and sad! I'll tell you a secret, Laetitia, sometimes I used to put my hair - so - and arrange a scarf -so - and pretend I was her, locked up in a castle, receiving a faithful servant who had swum the moat at midnight and climbed a rope to my window to give me a message from my true friends."

"The ink would have run while he was swimming."

"So it would. No, it was wrapped in oilskin… how I wish I had lived then, or if I had to live now it could be in some far off place like Italy."

"Italy? For the warm winters? Ah no, you are thinking of castles, and monks, and ghosts and mountain torrents and robber chieftains and caves… but have you not mountains and torrents a-plenty at home? Can you be quite sure that your own house is not haunted?"

"I do not think it would be easy for a house of seven children to be haunted. There is too much laughing and scampering and hiding in dark corners to share gingerbread and secrets."

"And yet it is an old house, is it not?"

"Two hundred years or more. But it looks too safe for ghosts with its wood sheltering it behind and its stout, round chimneys. You would laugh at the chimneys, but all the houses near home have them. Besides, I don't think that anyone who lived there was ever unhappy long enough for a ghost to come."

Laetitia turned her head away, and gazed out of the window. After a heavy pause, she said in a low voice, "How fortunate you are. .I wish I could say the same of my house – there is always some trouble here. I know that Papa is troubled about something, and Mama is often unwell and sadly disturbed…"

"And Frederick, your brother? Is he, too, unhappy?"

"I'm not sure. I doubt a young man of one and twenty would take a sister into his confidence. And besides, he is here so rarely. He is expected soon you know, and may bring some friends… perhaps when he is here all will be better. I am truly glad you are with me, Araminta. Even if all the whispers and hints are groundless-"

"What do you mean?"

"Nothing, nothing to care for, some of the maids have gone away in haste, and I have overheard talk of..well..of noises and lights when all are abed, and doors left open by no known hand… and such folly… You know how full of superstition servants can be."

"But perhaps there might be some strange-"

"Nonsense… we are becoming morbid ourselves; the autumn chills are eating into our minds. Would you care to try the pianoforte? We can sing some of the songs we learnt in York. And if it is still fine this afternoon, I will take you to explore the grounds."

When Lady Fenborough came into the room half an hour later she was delighted by the sweetness of the girls' singing, and remained with them the rest of the morning

Letter from Araminta to Louisa.

My dearest Louisa,

I awoke refreshed from the ardours of my journey and eager to explore. From my window I looked out over a well-planted park with number of deer grazing in the distance. As Celestine was dressing my head she told me there had been deer in the park for centuries, according to one of the maids, but the herd had increased of late. They are not nearly so pretty as our own deer, and not as cautious as they should be. I do not think they would survive well in our steep and tangled woods.

On Celestine's advice I put on my figured muslin with the pink ribbons and I must own I felt quite elegant with my new hairstyle and the enamelled bracelet I had for my birthday. Laetitia was in a striped white and green fabric in a style I had not seen before, with a beautiful jewelled comb, She looks far more of a fully-grown young lady than I do, I fear, for all I am the taller. Yet after a little strangeness we freely exchanged the sacred memories of our youthful friendship. She has a handsome little dog, who put me in mind of our dear Shep, though she would be ashamed to laze the day away on a sofa, even though it is covered in pink satin. But begone , melancholy! I did not come away to pine for home and family, but to see new sights, renew old friendships and perhaps make new ones. Laetitia's Mama is most stately and slender. She is not as tall as our mother, and even if she is more elegantly dressed, she has a look of uncertainty and ill-health that I would be loath to see in my own parent.

But I intend to tell you about our walk this afternoon, Laetitia had promised to show me the grounds if it was fine, so about two o'clock we set out along a broad drive edged with lime trees. In a few minutes we were walking down towards water, glimpsed through the trees. Laetitia called it "the lake" but it was to my mind more a small tarn. Yet allowances must be made for those who have never seen Windermere nor gazed across it to the lofty peaks of Langdale!

I own I was astonished to hear that the lake had been constructed by Laetitia's grandfather, who had also caused the river through his land to be changed to a canal, to fall down through a series of cascades, which was very ingenious work, and the water makes a most impressive sound as it rushes down. I admired exceedingly, but with an inward sigh for the little wild waterfalls of the wood near home. There were a number of other small lakes, cut most symmetrically on shapes like half moons, with swans on them, and surrounded by smooth lawns. These were not in clear view as the walks along the side of the valley were planted with stout yew hedges; but this was cut away in places so the passer-by could have a glimpse of the scene below. At the back of three artificial lakes, equipped with statues of - I think - Neptune and other sea-gods was a Greek Temple in neat golden stone, with pillars and steps before it. Laetitia told me it had been intended as a temple for Hercules, but after his father's death her father had designated a Temple of Piety, dedicated to the shade of his father. A Temple on one's land seems to me strange and pagan – and can you imagine Tom dedicating a temple to Papa!

After a while we went by a winding path up a little hill, again artificial and built, so it is said - perhaps with malice - to prevent the owner of the neighbouring house from looking upon the elegant water gardens. Truly, to build it was a prodigious labour- but how much better a designer of hills, dear sister, is God than man! However, from a little seat on the summit we looked across to what is, for me, the glory of this place – the Abbey. Even though the roof is fallen and the tower silent, though none sing in the choir or walk hands clasped and heads bowed through the cloister, the whole edifice breathes of the life of the past, the days of chivalry and crusades.

What unfortunate young woman , banished to the cloister by a cruel and avaricious father determined to prevent her marriage to the brave, poor man she loved, may have passed her sad days within these walls ! Perhaps even bricked up to starve to death for daring to attempt a flight to her beloved, waiting in the woods with a white palfrey!

The very ivy on the tower, the broken crosses, the tumbled blocks of stone, speak to me of a vanished enchantment. How I longed to rush down the hill and wander among those stones, imagining the monks and nuns at their labour and touching the rough Gothic carvings! But alas, this cannot be. When I asked Laetitia if we could go down the Abbey she pointed out a great ugly wall and told me sadly that the Abbey did not belong to her estate, but was owned by the inhabitants of the nearby hall. I am sure they must be horrid people, or they would let us walk there. Laetitia thinks her father would dearly love to own the ruins, but so far they are not ours, and there is no way, she tells me, that we can approach any nearer.

We left the hill and crossed the water by a cunningly constructed rustic bridge. Laetitia was for returning along the other side of the canal, but I spied a path up into the trees and pressed forward along it, with more eagerness than courtesy, I fear. As we walked along the ridge at the top of the bank, which was all wooded, we found an eight-sided tower with pinnacles and parapets in the Gothic manner, a pleasing modern compliment to the noble pile we had just beheld.

Beyond this tower lay a dark opening into the hillside, and thither the pathway led. For a moment I hesitated, for the darkness within was complete, but Laetitia walked strongly forward so I followed with few qualms, since she has never been one to court peril or inconvenience. Sure enough, a few paces brought us to a turn in the tunnel, light showed ahead, and we shortly emerged lower down the hillside and so returned to the lake. The path continued by the river along the valley, but Laetitia felt we had walked far enough and suggested we could ride that way some other day. I would have liked to go on in the late sunlight but must needs submit cheerfully to the wishes of my hostess. Indeed, when I looked down our skirts and patterns were thick with mud.

On our return to the house we saw a groom leading off two horses, one a very fine bay. "Ah!" cried Laetitia, "that is Frederick's. He must have come home!" She said this with a look of greater animation than I had yet seen in her, and I honoured her the more for her love of her brother. We met at dinner, but all I can tell you is that he is dark-haired and most handsome, not unlike that noble highwayman that you and I concealed in the icehouse away from the dragoons when we little! You remember how we stole a pasty from the kitchen for him, and when we got to the icehouse were obliged to eat it ourselves. Frederick spoke little, and mainly to his father and the friend he had brought with him, about their plans for hunting on the morrow. He is called William Charlton, and looks good-humoured and well-bred, though not exactly handsome. To Laetitia her brother spoke kindly, calling her "little Letty" and he asked me how I did. I could see he was very fatigued, and am not inclined to judge him as a conversationalist by this evening.

With dearest love to you and all (including Shep)

Araminta.

P.S. I can not put away from my mind the picture of the Abbey ruins. I do believe I saw a low place in the ugly

16

dividing wall, no higher than farmer Lowden's wall we scrambled over years ago after green apples. But I am a young lady now, and must not scramble over walls.

As I write this in my room the moon is almost full, and is picking out the trees and pathways. It is almost light enough to see one's way; it would be quite light enough but for the clouds drifting across the moon's face. Louisa, I must wander among those enchanting ruins. How delightful they would be in the pale beams of the frosty moon! Louisa dear, keep my counsel, I do not yet know what I shall attempt. Whatever comes, Laetitia shall know nothing, for I cannot ask her to disregard her parents' clear wishes. For the same reason, dear, dear sister, make sure our mother does not read this. How I wish you were here with me! Goodnight. A.

Thursday October 14th

My dear Louisa,

I little thought when I left off my letter of yesterday and sent it to the post that I should have an affair of such alarming portent to describe to you as now follows. Often we have spoken lightly of strange and supernatural beings, and inclined to scorn those who give them credence. My heart now smites me for the way we mocked poor Tabitha when she swore she had been followed home by a huge, silent black dog with eyes of flame, and told her she had filled us with so many nursery tales that at last she believed them! Indeed, I am terribly agitated. I do not know what I have seen, and I am not sure I wish to. I will try to tell you a collected story, as if you had been at my side. I am half ashamed at my agitation; take care I do not become a laughingstock within my own family.

Well, as I said in my last, we did not finish exploring the grounds yesterday. We could not ride this morning as the horses were all required for hunting and the carriage. I had hoped we would walk again this afternoon but as Laetitia and I were planning to set out her mother sent for her, sending a message to me that she must detain her daughter for the rest of the afternoon. So Celestine and I took the walk I had intended with my friend.

We found the lake again, and turning left instead of right, began to follow the path beside the water which as it emerges from the lake over one last fall, is permitted again to follow its own channel with what bends, rocks and eddies it will. The water runs merrily, as if glad to be free of its restraints, down a winding valley. The path also winds, now one side of the stream, now the other, carried by many little bridges. It reminds me of the figures of a country dance, with path and river as partners meeting and turning away all the way down the set.

We had not advanced far along the path when we saw, on a low-lying grassy plot within a bend on the far side of the river, a most curious edifice. It seemed to consist of about a dozen roughly-dressed stone blocks, each twice the height of a man, arranged in a circle many yards across. They looked like nothing so much as the picture on the study wall at home of the Druids' Temple at Stone Henge, except that there were no stones laid crosswise atop the others. And in the centre, like an altar lay one huge, grim block, like the one where the Stone Henge Druids were wont to sacrifice a beautiful maiden to the rising sun at midsummer. I pointed this out to Celestine who told me she had heard of these circles in other places too. She thinks there may be one near Keswick, far to the north of us. But, like me, she was astonished to see one so near. We were not sure whether it might have been set there of recent years, or if it came down from the dawn of history, and I determined to ask Laetitia about it when I returned to the house.

As we carried on down the valley we forgot the stones, entranced by the leaves chasing across the grass and the busy squirrels scampering round the tree trunks hunting for nuts, but ever wary to keep their distance from us human intruders. Celestine had some pieces of biscuit in her pocket, so we scattered crumbs around and sat down as still as - I was going to say mice, but stiller - as still as old pussy when she sits waiting for the birds, and after a time, first one, then another tiny creature sprang cautiously forward and took up a morsel. I love to see them eat, sitting up, holding the crumbs in their hands like men and constantly turning quick eyes and ears, alert for peril. At last we laughed and they fled, their bushy tails whisking in the air.

After a while clouds obscured the sun, and we returned, fearful lest we be caught by a shower and my fine new walking dress suffer harm. We pressed forward with all speed, but as it came on to rain heavily we sheltered under an oak tree by the water, near to the spot where we had seen the ring of stones. As I peered through the sheeting rain my eyes made out what seemed to be a patch of light brown on the dark cliffs behind, almost like a piece of cloth. Then it was moved aside from within, and I saw it was a curtain made of deerskin across the mouth of a little cave. Thence emerged the strange figure of a tall weather beaten man, with a long unkempt beard and white locks flowing beneath his shoulders. He was clad in a robe that had once been white, across his shoulders was a deerskin and around his waist a curiously –wrought girdle. In his hand he carried a goblet of metal. He came down to the stream, dipped it, and drank. As he raised his head he looked across the river and saw us beneath the trees. His eyes met mine. It fixed me with a malignant stare! Drawing himself to his full height he thrust out a skinny arm and pointed at me, then proceeded to cry out in words I could not comprehend, but in tones I understood only too well. It was a cry of vengeful malediction! My blood froze within my veins. I stole a glance at Celestine and clasped her hand. She turned and smiled, and to my horror I saw no dread in her eyes or pallor upon her cheeks. I could not speak. She had seen nothing!

I looked across the river again. The man had disappeared. A fit of trembling seized me. Celestine put the spare shawl she had been carrying round my shoulders and asked me how I did. As I struggled to speak we saw a servant from the house approaching, carrying umbrellas. Thankful I had not betrayed myself, I endeavoured to appear calm and eager only to gain the refuge of the house. We hastened home, and you may guess I had no peace from Celestine until I had changed my clothes and warmed myself thoroughly by the fire. Even then I was curiously reluctant to ask her what she had seen. I may have imagined the whole! I do not wish her to think me still full of childish fantasies, and she seemed so unaware of ought amiss. I determined to speak to Laetitia as soon as I could.

Alas, when I descended to the drawing room it was to be told that she was fatigued and had a slight chill, so would not rejoin the party that evening. So for a while I listened languidly to the conversation, placid to all appearances, but with what underlying turmoil you alone, dear Louisa, can guess. Eventually Frederick entered the room, and we fell into conversation. After he had told me of his success in hunting he asked me how I had spent the day, and I told him where we had been, and asked about the stone circle.

"Is it really old, or has it been put there of recent years?" I asked him.

He looked at me gravely, and told me it was very old indeed, from before the time of Julius Caesar and the Ancient Romans. "Indeed,"he said " Druids have worshipped on that spot for three thousand years, despite turmoils and persecution."

"And… were there ever sacrifices on that stone?"

"Every year, seven maidens of noble birth were sacrificed throughout the centuries, to please the destructive anger of the sun, The rites were brought to an end in the time of the monks. They, of course had little love for the Druids, whose powers were so much greater than their own. When the monks first came, they destroyed all they could find of the Druids' sacred mistletoe, and fought unceasingly to stop the sacrifices."

"So when was it the last Druid lived here?"

"About five hundred years ago. It is said that the last Druid was abducted by the Prior of the Abbey, and offered the choice of death or recantation. He tore away from his captors, and flung himself down from the top of the tower to his death. He is said to have been a very tall man with a noble beard."

It was, you may imagine, with great difficulty I asked the next question. "What… what kind of clothes do you think he would have worn in those days?"

"Oh, a long white robe with a deerskin, and a mystic jewelled belt. They say he fell clutching a priceless sacred goblet, which could not be found when his lifeless corpse was gathered up by the cruel monks, and cast to rot in the midst of his own stone circle."

The room swam around me. Frederick caught my arm and gazed intently at me. "The story frightens you? Nay, there is no need to fear and grow pale, 'tis but a story." Gradually my breath came back, and I contrived to smile at him, yet I fear it was but a poor smile.

"It is true," he went on, "that there have been rumours from time to time. It is said that over the years he has been seen within the circle he tended with such devotion – and that such appearance has signified a terrible doom both to those who have seen him and to those whom the vision is confided. But what of that? He has not been seen in my lifetime. I.."

Araminta broke off and started out of the window at the bare branches lashing against the moon. If only she could have seen Laetitia, and found out from her if Frederick was always to be trusted. But no! How could she ask her? Not only would it be discourteous to question her brother's reliability, but suppose what he said was true? What had Laetitia been saying about the unhappiness in her home? She could not risk bringing upon her the terrible doom she may herself have incurred. What would Louisa – no, wait. The letter must not be sent! Louisa and her family must not be destroyed also. She must bear this terrible burden quite alone, but how could she? What did it all mean?

When Celestine came in to brush her hair she found her young mistress huddled before the fire, her head in her hands, sobbing and trembling. On the floor beside lay the letter she had been writing, and she did not seem to hear the maid's anxious questions. Celestine had been with the family for twelve of her twenty-three years. She had been sent with Araminta as her maid, certainly, but as they were leaving Mrs Lewthwaite had said quietly, "Celestine, it is a long way for my daughter to be going away from home. Watch over her carefully, preserve her from any harm her elegant friends or eager nature may bring upon her. If you are seriously alarmed at any time, write to me." So she had no hesitation in picking up the pages and taking them over to the candle. Relieved to see by the hand and the greeting that the letter was neither from nor to a clandestine admirer, she read through to find the source of her charge's trouble. As she read she smiled, and suppressing a chuckle she cried out.

"Minta, dear child, what a goose you are!"

Araminta looked up and saw her with the letter. "Don't read that! I order you- put it down at once!"

"Too late. I have read the whole story."

"But the curse! Now you will be fated too, and all on account of my folly!"

Celestine composed herself and spoke more gently to comfort her.

"I am afraid, my dear that Master Frederick has been amusing himself at your expense. Of course I saw the man too. I did not mention it because I could see you did not wish to speak of him."

"And did you hear that terrible curse in his ancient tongue? My blood ran cold to hear it."

"Listen to me. I know that was no curse in the Druids' language, for their ancient tongue is like the speech of the Welsh. When I was a little girl I once spent the summer at my great grandparents' cottage in a Breton village. While I was there a fishing boat from Wales was driven to the shore in a gale, and I met and spoke with the Welshmen who had no language but their own,"

"H…how then did you understand them?"

"The Welsh speak very like the Bretons. I could speak in the Breton tongue with my great grandparents, and these strangers, although they used many words I did not know, could be understood for the most part by the whole village. They were with us for some days mending the boat and I never tired of listening to them. Great Grandfather used to spend the day helping them while I played nearby, fishing for shrimps and jumping in the pools. And so I know that the man today was not speaking the Welsh language; and I know also that he is a being of flesh and blood."

"How can you be so sure? I am not a child, do not try to reassure me as if I was a baby."

Celestine took up the brush and unpinned Araminta's hair. As she brushed she went on. "I own I was curious about the man, so while you were asking Frederick I was asking someone who has worked here for some time. He tells me the circle was built about twenty years ago – before his time – and that some years ago this man was hired to live in the cave, and from time to time to act the part of the Druid of the place."

"But why? And where did he come from?"

"A troupe of travelling actors had been performing nearby and lodged over night in a barn in the village. This man was left behind with a fever; the rest of the party, except for his wife, went on. Then his wife took ill from him and died quickly. The owner of the barn tended this man back to health. He stayed in the area and tried to find himself some work. His Lordship took a fancy to have a Druid in his circle and engaged the man to become the ancient Druid for a term of years in exchange for an annuity in his old age. I suppose the master thought it would be appropriate to adorn his stone circle with a Druid. Other houses have their ghosts and monks!"

"You are sure of this?"

"I gather he comes in every so often after dark into the kitchen and is given a good meal and a warm by the fire, for he has a cold and lonely position. He is only another servant, like the rest, but with a strange duty."

Each thought in silence of her informant that evening. Then Araminta pink cheeked, tore up her letter and threw it in the fire. As she was being prepared for bed she said quietly, "I do not admire Frederick for mocking me in that way. How he must have laughed to himself! I should be sorry to see Tom behave so little like a gentleman. And yet he looked so earnest. I will take care not to let myself be teased again. You are quite, quite sure?"

"Quite sure, miss. Shall I leave the candle alight by your bed?"

"No there is no need. Goodnight Celestine."

"Goodnight, miss. Sleep well."

When Celestine returned later to tend the fire she stood for a long time watching the sleeping girl, shielding the candle flame with her fingers.

Friday October 15th

The next morning Araminta wrote home more briefly.

My dearest Louisa,

I was glad to hear all your news. The new gown sounds delightful and how clever of Shep to have had twelve puppies. You will be happy to have Tom and his friends with you. I hope they may stay a long time.

I have seen more of Frederick and had further conversation with him. My dear, I do not think he can be an altogether agreeable character , much as I was prepared to admire and esteem him for his sister's sake, for she always speaks of him with such admiration. I own he is very pleasing indeed as to person and address, and I had looked forward to our further acquaintance with much pleasure, but I fear the old saying 'Handsome is as handsome does' may apply to him. I think him inconsiderate at times.

This morning Laetitia took me to see the aviary. As we made our way thither along the winding path Frederick approached us, walking quickly, with a flushed countenance. He made as if to pass without speaking, hurriedly pushing past us and forcing me to tread in the mire. Laetitia called out to him, so he turned round and gave us good morning. She said we were going to visit the aviary and asked him if he would join us. He refused brusquely: "I will not, It's a stupid place, and all the birds in there want their necks wringing." He made off. Laetitia did not reply but I felt her hand on my arm trembling.

The aviary is a long, airy room, with large cages on either side. Trees in Chinese pots are growing inside them, providing perches for a variety of colourful little parakeets with blue and green breasts, and pretty golden canary birds. The room was warm; I suppose to cheer the little exiles with memories of their own sun-warmed forests. One of the maids was sweeping up birdseed from the floor. "Why Betty!" cried Laetitia, "are you not done feeding them yet?"

"No miss. I have been delayed this morning. I have still to feed the new arrivals. Would you like to come and see them?" She led us down the room to a smaller cage where two lilac-breasted parakeets sat huddled on a branch. Betty entered the cage to put fresh water in a porcelain dish and scatter bird seed. We admired their unusual plumage and hoped they would soon feel sufficiently at home to fly and chirp quite happily again.

Most of our talk must remain in confidence as we spoke with the complete unreserve of true friendship. Later she asked me if I had seen the Druid at the stone circle on my walk the day before. One of the unusual devices in the park is a miniature Stone Henge, with a retainer dressed as a druid! I had indeed seen both, and found them most impressive.

Laetitia said they had been there as long as she could remember. "When I was a little girl," she said, "I used to be terrified of him. It was all Frederick's teasing. If I had anything he wanted, a new ball or a puppy, he would tell me that unless I let him have it for a while the Druid would come and get me, snatching me from my bed. My nurse would not be able to protect, for he would come while she slept. I suppose he did not know how he terrified me, for I often lay awake rigid with fear, awaiting his tread upon the staircase, and hearing it in fancy a thousand times. But as boys are never afraid of anything I am sure he could not have understood the pain he caused me." I said nothing to this, but knowing how frightened little Charlie was last autumn when the great storm crashed through the trees, I was not inclined so readily to acquit Frederick of an understanding of terror on account of his sex alone. This evening he was in a much more pleasing mood; he has offered to ride with us one day soon to us the picturesque Brimham Rocks, a few miles across the moors from where we are staying.

I shall write again when I have more news. Please give my love to the whole family,

Araminta.

* * *

She sealed the letter then rang for Celestine to see her to bed, saying she was fatigued and wished to retire early. Yet she lay awake for a long while, thinking of the conversation in the aviary. Laetitia had considered there was some serious trouble afoot; her mother had spoken of Frederick's affairs with trepidation. Both wondered why he had not brought with him the friend he had intended to accompany him. This friend, a Captain John Masterman, had been to visit several times before and Frederick had just been with him on his estate in Northamptonshire. There had been a niece among the company and Laetitia thought Frederick might have been paying her some attention. But something had caused a break with the whole family; Frederick had left there suddenly and had come home with a hitherto unknown fellow guest as companion. Araminta wondered if he had perhaps incurred heavy gaming debts, but Laetitia either knew no more or was unwilling to speak.

She was now wide awake and the full moon glared in at the window, picking out details of the bedclothes and jars on the mantelpiece. The fire was dying, and there was no sound anywhere. She left her bed and moved to the window. All was still and peaceful outside, while a weight of sorrow seemed to seep into her from the very walls of the room. Taking her watch over to the window, she saw it was two o'clock. There were no lights showing on her side of the house and no glimmer under the door. Quietly opening the door to Celestine's little room she listened to her regular breathing. There was no other sound. She was oppressed by the silence of the great mansion, and thinking of the empty rooms around. She made to enter Celestine's room and arouse her for the sake of a familiar voice, But Celestine was deeply asleep and she would not disturb her like a small child calling for her nurse when lonely and afraid.

She looked out of the window, towards the walls of the distant abbey picked out in the harsh moonlight. Then she turned and resolutely got back into bed, pulling the blankets up over her head. She would try to forget about all this strange formal splendour around her close her eyes tight and think about home, remember happy things. There was the evening in June when Tom was home and walked with her and Louisa to the hayfields. She fixed her mind on this …what each was wearing, what they had talked about, followed the path to the fields step by step, tasting the scent of the new-mown hay. As she retraced her steps in that cheerful company she lost her restless agitation and drifted away into a gentle dream.

The dream had changed. She was still walking but it was dark now. The wind was whipping her cloak round her ankles and she was on a strange path. She reached down to feel Shep – but she had run off. Tom and Louisa were not there. Where could they be? Where was their hayfield? She suddenly knew she was walking along the path to the abbey ruins and stopped, bewildered. Was this part of her dream or was it real? She reached out to a tree beside the path and felt the rough bark graze her fingers- but that might be in the dream too. Her feet had brought her to the foot of the wall behind which rose the abbey.

There was a light in the ruins, moving at the height one would carry a candle or lantern. It moved along the outside of the church wall and paused near the entrance. Then it flared up for a moment, to show it was held by a hand emerging from a heavy woollen sleeve and flickered on a cowled, bent head.

Araminta was too frightened to move or cry out. She dare not look again towards the church but turned and rushed blindly along the paths, not knowing where she ran, so long as it was away from that terrible sight. Once as she paused for breath she thought she heard above the thumping in her breast the sound of footsteps and a swishing robe behind her. She ran on again then, oblivious of the stones and patches of ice on the paths, forgetting where she was and where she might find safety. Then with a gasp of relief, she saw ahead of her the Temple of Piety. She rushed into it - here was something safe and solid, reassuringly of her own day and age. She would shelter there to regain her breath and return to the house quickly. They need never know she had left her room. She entered thankfully between the pillars. In a patch of moonlight on the floor not four feet from her lay the figure of the Druid, stiff and lifeless, its cup grasped in its gnarled hand. As the vision spun round and she sank to the floor, she heard again the footsteps behind her.

Celestine woke suddenly, She lay for a moment trying to collect her thoughts and discover why she had woken. She saw the open door to Araminta's room and went through to see if she had cried out in her sleep. That foolish young man's nonsense might well have given her bad dreams. Then she saw the room was empty. She felt the bed- still warm. Could she have walked in her sleep? When Araminta had had a fever as a little girl, she had once or twice walked by night, suddenly awakening frightened and uncertain where she was, and again when her little brother Samuel died. Glancing round the room she saw some clothes were missing. Asleep or awake, she had dressed and gone out. Hastily putting on her own clothes, she followed down the stairs. She saw the outer door, tried it, and slipped out. A recent footprint in the mud showed she had gone that way. Whatever the foolish girl was doing, awake or asleep, she must be found and brought back without scandal or disturbance. She would hardly have gone back to the scene of her fright the day before, so she turned at the lake towards the Abbey ruins. She hurried down the path for what seemed a long time, and suddenly saw a dark figure running across a side path. It was Araminta, and she seemed terrified. Celestine followed quietly, not daring to call out. If she was walking in her sleep a sudden awakening could be dangerous. She saw her enter the Temple of Piety. When she followed she found her unconscious on the stone floor, before noticing with a shudder the unmistakably dead body of the strange Druid. Araminta's need conquered Celestine's fear and revulsion. She knelt beside her, shielding her from the hideous sight, and loosened her clothing.

Araminta's eyes opened, and as sense returned, so did horror. "Celestine, did you see him too?"

"Yes I can see him too. Don't try to get up yet, stay quiet for a minute. There is nothing to be done for this poor man. He is dead. I will look after you and take you back to bed. Do you remember how you came to be here?"

" I don't know. I was dreaming about a walk at home with Shep and the family and then it all changed, and I found I was on the path near the abbey ruins. And the I saw – no, I can't tell you it is too frightful, But I turned away and ran back towards the house. When I saw this place I thought I would be safe and here, here on the floor... You see that thing behind us?"

"We can do nothing for the poor man. Perhaps, he has laid violent hands on himself. He can be left until the morning.. What we must do now is to get you back into the house without disturbance." Celestine spoke calmly but her heart seemed to squirm inside her, for she thought she had seen something like a male figure lurking in the shadows. She helped Araminta to her feet, and they moved towards a stone bench, but as she saw the body again, her legs gave way under her. Celestine struggled to support her, and before she realised what was happening, she felt another pair of arms take the girl's dead weight and settle her on the bench.

"Don't be afraid, Celestine, it's only me."

She recognised Porrott, the manservant with whom she had talked the evening before. "Whatever are you doing here?" she whispered.

"I might well ask you the same. I cannot suppose you at least to be after a hare or a pheasant. And you would not expect me to open myself to that kind of accusation, but I promise you I am doing no harm."

"But there is a dead man, and you are out where you should not be."

"You must decide for yourself if you are to trust me. I think we have little choice but to be allies. It seems to me we should all seek to avoid a hue and cry. Whatever have you both been doing to be found with a recently dead man?"

"Miss Araminta has from time to time walked in her sleep, and I found she had left her room and followed her. I have just come upon her, but it would be folly indeed to imagine she would have anything to do with this death!. She cannot bear to see a mouse killed and will open a window to let even a wasp escape."

Porrott smiled awkwardly, "Indeed I can hardly picture either of you as a blood-stained desperado. We had best get her home as fast as we can. In the morning I will come this way, and if no-one else has reported this sad body, will raise the alarm then. Let us be sure we have left nothing behind." Despite Celestine's impatience he insisted on looking carefully all around, picking up a ribbon knot which had fallen from Araminta's dress and sweeping away with his hands the mud they had brought in on their shoes. Then he picked up the semi-conscious Araminta and the three hastened back to the house. "Can you manage her alone?" he asked when they were inside the hall. "Wait here, I will rouse Betty and send her to you. She is a sensible and discreet girl."

Celestine waited a long time in the silent hall. She was beginning to wonder if she could manage to take her mistress to her room alone when she saw a figure come downstairs and heard a soft whisper "Celestine? Porrott asked me to come and help you with your mistress. Whatever has she been doing?"

"No harm, I can tell you. She has been subject to walking in her sleep. Indeed, in some ways she is still a child, and innocence itself. Foolish she may be at times, but never wicked. Please let us get her quietly abed."

With some difficulty this was done. Celestine brought the cover from her own bed and passed the rest of the night in an easy chair in Araminta's room when she had given her a sleeping draught.

Saturday October 16th

"Celestine, … Celestine … oh what a terrible dream I have had!"

It was now full day, and Araminta struggled to her elbow, lurching upward through layers of oblivion. Then she saw that Celestine was carefully brushing caked mud from the skirt of the dress she had worn in that dream, and felt the tangles in her hair and stiffness in her legs and neck. Celestine stopped brushing and looked at her. She did not speak but her look forced Araminta to consider that it might all be real.

"Did - that- happen, last night, or was it just a nightmare?" but as she asked the question she knew the answer. "Whatever can we do? I want to go home. No I don't, I can't."

Celestine moved over to the side of the bed and took her hand. "I see you recall it all now. Yes, you went out last night in your sleep and I found you in the Temple and there we found the body of a man."

"It was the Druid! I can still see him when I close my eyes. He seemed to be looking at me with those sightless eyes, fixed staring wide open. Will he ever leave me alone?":

Celestine brought warm water and a soft cloth and a soft cloth and began to wash her face. "Of course he will. You know he is not really there, just a horrible recollection."

"I think I must have wandered in my sleep like I used to. I was so frightened when I woke and so cold. I was right up close to the abbey wall. Suddenly I saw this light – and there was something like an aged monk holding it.. I was terrified and fled, and all the while I heard steps behind me, and when I found the Temple I thought I would be safe. But how did you manage to bring me back here? I am sure I could not have walked, indeed, I have a half-recollection of being carried – but by whom?" Celestine explained what help had been at hand, and how Porrott would " discover" the body himself later that morning.

"I will send word that you are a little indisposed and will remain in your room for a while. We will have some food sent up from the kitchen and remain here until the discovery has been made public. Once that has happened, our main trouble is at an end. I see no reason why last night's wanderings should be made public."

"No indeed! I would not care for Laetitia, and even less for her family, to know how week and foolish I had been. Nor my own parents. Surely there is no need for them to know of this. "

Celestine had been troubled as to her duty in this respect. To tell them would surely lead to Araminta's abrupt summons home, and perhaps unpleasant rumours for her in the neighbourhood; reputation once lost is not easily recovered. And yet …. Araminta gazed pleadingly at her, looking as fresh and harmless as a young puppy. "I can see no immediate need to write home; the man's death, though sad, can not be in any way a threat to us."

" I suppose you are right and we must stay up here a while, for I am sure I cannot bear to see anyone just yet and behave as if nothing had happened, but what a tedious and troublesome wait it will be. How can I contrive to find out what is happening? When will I know it is safe to go down among them?"

"Once you are dressed you could come through and sit in my room. There the window overlooks the courtyard, so we shall see the comings and goings beneath us." Even if this does not give us the information we want, she thought, it will provide some distraction for her.

So maid and mistress sat by the window. At first the yard was empty. Then came a kitchen maid with a pail of greasy water to throw away. As she returned a well-fed black and white cat sidled through the door she had left ajar, settled itself into a patch of sunlight, stretched, reaching out with all its claws and began to wash itself thoroughly. Araminta watched every movement with desperate concentration; the cat had just raised a hind paw to its ear when a shadow fell across the animal. Cat and girl turned to look for its source. A cart had clattered into the yard, and the young carter was fastening the reins to a post. He was tall, and moved with a hurried, angry walk. As he reached the kitchen door it opened, and out ran one of the young maids. Araminta thought it was the girl she had seen feeding the birds-what was her name, Susan? No, Betty. She and the carter were talking quickly to one another; both were agitated. Suddenly he grasped her by the arm and rushed her into the kitchen. Had he, then, made the fateful discovery? But surely no cart would go that way. Yet he might have met the other man, the one who was to find the body, and come back with the news.

She could hear sounds from below, clearly there was some disturbance but not so much as she would have expected had the news of the body been reported. The courtyard was again still. The cat moved to the other hind leg in his spot in the sun. How she envied that cat, with no concern but keeping in the sun and being comfortable. After a while, the door burst open again. The young man was still holding on to Betty, but in his hand there was a bundle. This he flung into the cart, then he helped Betty into the seat at the front, untied the horses, turned the cart and made off at good speed. As they rattled under the archway Betty looked back; Araminta saw her face was red and thought she was weeping. What could be made of that? How fierce the man had looked! His manner was more that of a ruffian than a decent workman. And how unhappy the girl had seemed. Surely she was not being taken away against her will.

Celestine was also troubled by what she had seen. She fervently hoped it had no connection with the help she had given the night before. It certainly looked as if she had been summarily turned away by the housekeeper for some transgression.

Half an hour passed. Three maids came to the pump for water and stood chatting a while until a sharp knocking on the kitchen window made them start guiltily and struggle back with their heavy pails. As the door opened a voice could be heard scolding, words gushing out as fiercely as the water the grooms were now pumping to take to the stables. Porrott strolled into the yard and spoke to one of them. They went over towards the stables together.

"There he is," murmured Celestine. "I suppose he will take Master Frederick's horse for exercise by the Temple and bring back the news. Araminta blushed to think that this unknown young man had seen her at a disadvantage and carried her so far. Celestine sensed some part of her thought. "I told him you were sleepwalking, as you used to when you were younger." She was not, however, sure that he believed her, any more than she believed he had been poaching.

The morning crawled by. "Surely he must have got there by now! 'Tis but a few minutes' ride!"

"But he must not ride straight there, as if to an appointment. He must go one of the ways he is accustomed to take the animals for exercise, and delay his discovery until he is on his way back."

It was more than another half hour before the thud of hooves sounded on the drive, distant at first but building up inexorably until horse and rider appeared and reined suddenly. The horse was restless and frightened, and Porrott himself looked pale. He leapt down, shouted to a groom to take the horse, and walked inside quickly. Neither of the watchers spoke. The door opened again, and the master of the house whom Araminta had seen only briefly at dinner, appeared fastening his cape. He shouted orders and set off on horseback with Porrott, followed by six men on foot who carried an old door and a grey blanket.

The vigil at the window was broken by the sound of running feet. The door of Araminta's room burst open and Laetitia rushed in , crying, "Minta! Minta! The most terrible thing has happened! Oh Minta, where are you?"

Araminta returned to her room and Laetitia flung herself at her, collapsing in raucous sobs. Celestine joined them: "Why, Miss Laetitia, whatever can be the matter? Just sit down quietly and let me give you a glass of water. We can't hear a word when you are crying like that."

Laetitia allowed herself to be put in an armchair and given a drink She tried to speak, but it was some minutes until she was sufficiently calm to be understood. Araminta sat beside her on a footstool, to all appearances perplexed and concerned for her friend.

"What is it, Letty? Can you not tell me?"

"I...I have just heard it. I overheard Porrott speaking to Papa. The study door was open and I was just passing. When I heard him begin I had to stay and hear what it was. Porrott says that the Druid has been found - dead - in the Temple where we walked the other day."

Araminta's hand flew to her mouth, and she threw Celestine a desperate glance.

"A terrible shock for you indeed," put in Celestine. "And yet I recall he was an aged man. Might he not have wandered there in the night, and perished from the exertion, or even the night time cold?"

"No, no. That was Papa's suggestion. I could not well hear Porrott's reply, but I heard Papa's next words. " You mean he may have laid violent hands on himself!" Then the groom said , "He or another." I am sure nobody could wish to kill such a harmless old man. He must himself have – 0h but it is terrible! He has always been there in the park

42

from my earliest recollections. I never knew his name. But how can someone you have known all your life be gone so suddenly? I thought I cared nothing about him; I certainly never sought him out to speak to him, and yet he is gone."

Both girls wept together; one from shock and the other from both sympathy and relief. Celestine stole back into her own room and saw the party return with the humped blanket borne upon the door. The master followed them into the outbuilding. Porrott held the door for him, and just before following him inside he glanced up for a moment, looking for Celestine's window. He found it, and looked directly at her; a glance full of meaning which she could not interpret.

Returning to tend the fire in the main room she heard "Araminta, promise you won't go home yet awhile. I implore you. I must soon go down to Mama, but I must wait until Papa has had opportunity to speak to her, then I must feign innocence until she tells me. I tremble for her; she is so sensitive to any breath of trouble that I fear this may bring on a fever; I cannot speak to my aunt, for she and I are almost strangers, and besides she is near her time. There is none I can confide in here but yourself."

"What of your brother, Frederick?"

"Only if he speaks to me of it first. Perhaps, some years ago.. but now he is... well, he is concerned with matters proper to young men and naturally has little time for anything else."

Araminta had been hoping to leave as soon as she could. The only way to be free from the terror which haunted her was to leave the place at once. And yet… flight had not served her well before. Would it not be intolerable never to know what had happened? All her life to wonder? Perhaps the truth was the only medicine that could heal the nightmare. And Laetitia, also, how often had she written to her vows of eternal love and friendship, vows she had never expected to be called upon to carry out. How could she go away to her cheerful home and leave her still more frightened and lonely, without even a Celestine to help her?

"Letty," she replied with an effort, " I must return if I am sent for, but I promise you that if I am permitted to do so, I will remain here with you a while. In a few days this will seem a matter of much less moment."

Betty was sullen and tearful as the cart joggled along the road. They had passed through the main gate some time before, but no word had been spoken since they left the kitchen. The carter pulled to the roadside and turned round. "Betty, Betty, have done with your crying. That was no fit place for you and I am taking you home. Your mother needs your help, for your grandmother is bedridden and needs tending constantly. They are longing to have you back, we all are. Betty, you are not angry with me are you?"

"Angry, John! When you burst into the house, drag me off to the housekeeper, tell her I am leaving and demand my wages! Then you stand over me while I pack my bag and put me up here so roughly that I am bruised and all with no word of explanation or excuse. Angry! Do you wonder that I am?"

"Betty, I saw it was no good place for you. I was afraid

you would come to harm there."

"What do you mean? Surely you do not believe the old wives' tales of ghosts and spirits?"

He laughed grimly. "No, I'd risk the ghosts. It's flesh and blood I fear, young hot blood. I saw the way he looked at you yesterday. We were talking in the yard, and the young master he rode by and stared at you in a way it is not fitting for a god fearing girl to be stared at by any. I went straight to your parents and told them you should come home."

" What did you say to them?"

"I told them you were not happy. I hope that is the truth. Come tell me Betty, you didn't–"

"If you hadn't been too angry to use your eyes when you saw him you'd have seen four new scratches under his chin. My work. He comes in when I'm feeding the birds and…"

"What did he say?"

"Say?. He wouldn't waste many words on the likes of you and me! He stared very boldly for a while, then made to catch hold of me in a way he should not, so I scratched his face for him and made to cry out. The next time I saw him he was in a cravat up to his lips and kept well away. You need have no fear, I can look after myself."

"I have been troubled by what I heard of him before, and when I heard he had returned I had to come and see how you were faring, And then I see - re you sure you have never encouraged him?"

"For shame, John! How dare you ask me such a thing? I want nothing to do with such lechers however highborn they may be. I thought better of you, who have known me all my life, than that you think I might be that kind of girl. I can walk home from here if that's what you think of me!"

"Betty, don't cry again please. I know you are not a wicked girl, but I have been so afraid for you. They say no maid is safe while Master Frederick is at home, and for all you say, you have not a man's strength. I did not mean to doubt you."

"And how am I to get another post, when I have left this one so suddenly?"

"Can you not stay at home a while and do some spinning work? Your family would be glad of you, and spinsters makes as good money as servants, and have neither master nor mistress. And I am managing to put a little by for the future. Perhaps, who knows, you need never seek for another post, but find a different kind of life as mistress of your own house?"

Betty said nothing beyond, "You had better drive on," but her manner of speaking caused John to sit up straighter and whistle a song to himself as he drove the horses on the long road home.

Tea was being taken in the drawing room. The fire was bright, the vista from the window crisp and attractive backed by a glowing sunset, which cast a warm light on the patterned carpet. The little lamp was keeping the kettle warm, muffins were in a silver dish. A tortoiseshell cat of ample proportions rubbed herself against her mistress and gazed intently at the heavy cream jug, waiting for her accustomed treat. The ladies of the house, Lady

Fenborough, Laetitia, her aunt and Araminta in their easy chairs enjoyed every comfort of body but none of spirit. The civilised apparatus of elegant furnishings, satisfying food and well-trained servants was useless in the wilderness within.

No word passed with reference to the morning's unsettling events, but tears were not far from Lady Fenborough's eyes, and the china cup in her slender hand rattled in its saucer; the loudest sound in a room where the fire glowed quietly and conversation proceeded unevenly. Aunt Margaret had been trying to keep up a suitable flow of talk with the girls but all subjects seemed within a few moments to be approaching that which must not be spoken of; should not be thought about, indeed, but thoughts cannot be mastered as easily as words.

Lord Fenborough had informed his wife of the discovery, and told her that there would be an inquest, as was inevitable in a case of sudden death. It was to be held on Monday the coroner had decided, and he himself would be required to give evidence as to identity. There was of course, no reason why any of the ladies should be required to attend. Araminta could not but think of the cold shed into which the body had been take. Was it still there? She could not ask; far better at any rate to assume it had been removed far away. She recalled his Lordship's kindly words, grateful that he had remembered her among the bustle of necessary tasks. "I am sorry this should happen while you were paying us a visit. I do hope you will still be able to enjoy your time with us. It is good that Laetitia should have a friend with her at this unhappy time." She watched the piled coals collapse into a red cave, in her mind composing the difficult letter she must write home. She must tell them what Lord Fenborough had said: that, and the lurking distrust implied by an earlier removal would probably cause her father to override her mother's qualms and insist on her remaining at Skells for some time.

Laetitia was fondling the cat, which had moved away from the fire when the coals sank down, rubbing along the side of her chin, listening intently for sounds in the hallway. She turned to the door a moment before anyone else heard it opening, as Frederick and his friend William came in.

The strained quietness in the room dispersed as the young men sat down by the fire. They had been out since early morning after pheasants and were ignorant of the day's events. Frederick was struck by his mother's wan appearance as she filled cups for the two of them.

"Whatever is wrong, Mother? You all look as cheerful as a set of mourners who've just learned they've been left out of the will. Someone's lapdog died? A tragedy with a careless maid and a new gown? A beloved china jar hit the parquet floor?"

Lady Fenborough turned her head away, and after a short silence his aunt replied, in rather cold tones, "Have you not heard then? We have had a rather trying experience this morning. One of the outdoor servants was unexpectedly found dead, in somewhat unusual circumstances."

"You make it sound most exciting. This is the most interesting thing that's happened here that I can remember,

William. Normally everything runs its predictable course until we are three parts dead of boredom. What exactly has happened? Have the head gardener and groom been engaged in a duel for the love of the dairymaid? Or has the housekeeper run amok with a hatchet and wrought carnage among the grooms?"

"Nay, Frederick, see, the ladies are indeed distressed," William murmured awkwardly, "we need to hear what has really taken place."

"Indeed we do. I am sorry, Mother, I should not have spoken so lightly. But do tell us the details if you do wish us to speculate on horrors."

Laetitia spoke hesitantly, her eyes still fixed on the cat's comfortable fur, "It has all been a terrible shock to us. That old man whom father set up as a druid has been found dead in the Temple of Piety. And even worse, they think perhaps his death was not natural - that someone - or even himself- "

"The poor fellow was half crazed you know, Letty. I should think nothing more likely but that he should make away with himself. But I am sorry to hear it. And found today, you say? At what time, and by whom?"

"One of the men, while he was exercising your horse, as I believe," said Araminta, since Laetitia seemed unable to form a sensible reply.

"A strange and sad event. But there, he has no kin to mourn him, and we must all die someday."

"But not by violence," remarked Aunt Margaret reproachfully.

"A better end I should think than many a long drawn out dying in bed, surrounded by lying doctors and greedy relatives. So that is why Papa seems so insistent to see us all in church tomorrow. He did not deign to explain; I expect he thought I knew. What a fool he must have thought me! Of course we must all be seen as a family before one and all. Mother, don't cry so, crying never brought anyone back, and ring for more muffins will you?"

Araminta had been watching Lady Fenborough and was surprised to see a flash - of interest? Alarm? – in her eye as she dutifully followed his instructions. She herself profoundly wished he had not used the words "bring him back". Where from, and to whom? How she hoped Celestine would suggest they slept together tonight!

Sunday October 17th

The church was packed for morning service. The rector smiled sardonically to himself, looking round during the singing of the Te Deum. The church was by no means over large for the village and the estate, yet on most Sundays there were far too many empty pews. This was only to be expected, when the heir himself attended so rarely when he was home, and Lady Fenborough was so often indisposed and thus unable to bear the chill of the stone walls (or in a hot dry spell, the stifling heat and proximity of the tenants.) And apart from those who followed the lead of the great family, many of the lower classes were not often seen, kept away by the Scylla of indifference or the Charybdis of Methodism, leaving him ,a man of learning, to read the services and preach to a small congregation of clodhoppers.

Today, though, slothful and sanctified had come together; not, he feared, because sudden death reminded them of the precariousness of life and the need to look to their latter end as because news could here be best heard and disseminated. The dead man himself had never been seen in church since the burial of his wife fifteen years previously – perhaps in view of his bizarre occupation this was hardly to be wondered at - but like them all, in he must come at last. And since it is more pleasing to preach to a full congregation, whatever their motives for attendance, he could not but feel a tinge of satisfaction that the old fellow had proved useful for once. "Nothing in his life became him like the leaving of it" - he pulled himself together; not suitable sentiments for the pulpit.

The Fenborough party sat in its high sided pew with the servants ranged behind. Their demeanour was sober and attentive, while behind the dignified faces thoughts swirled and rioted. Lord Fenborough hoped there would be no serious inconvenience. He certainly would not bother with a druid again, for he was heartily tired of the conceit. At least he would not now have to pay out that annuity. Perhaps after a decent interval he would demolish the stone circle itself, though undoubtedly it looked well on its site beside the stream. How ill Elizabeth was looking. He hoped she would not cause commotion by fainting. He glared warningly at her.

She was absorbed in self-pity. How cruel of Edward to insist that she came to church when she was so unwell and upset. What a long service it was today, surely the rector could have done without a sermon today, he must know that nobody would be listening. On the other hand, at the close of the service would come the worst ordeal of all, walking out past curious eyes and mocking whispers. It was easy enough for the young people, at their age one cares for nothing; and Margaret was so unfeeling too, sitting there with her husband, caring nothing for her sister's terrible embarrassment.

She judged her sister accurately, Margaret and her spouse shared the same thought: how soon would it be decent to curtail their visit. Her approaching confinement made it a duty for her to avoid troublesome situations whenever possible, and for the same reason it would fortunately be impossible for her to invite her niece to stay with her, desirable as it might otherwise have been for her to be taken out of the way, and removed from the society of that rather independent-looking young school friend of hers.

Frederick sat back with folded arms, glaring at his boots. That fool of a valet had not cleaned them properly, he could distinctly see a smear of mud on the instep. What a waste of a fine morning. There were a thousand things he could be doing. He had drunk far too much last night to have to be up to attend a ten o'clock service. It was all right for William, as a guest he could well be excused, but Father had brooked no denial from his son. There was some sense in the old man's thinking, though, it was necessary to display to all that this unfortunate incident in no way disconcerted them. Let the village people stare and murmur, what did it matter?

Laetitia was still shaken by her first encounter with death's invasion of her life of petty certainties. Someone who had always been about the place had gone. Next time she passed the stone circle there would be no point in looking across the water for him. And if death could stride through the park gates for one he could come for another. She glanced under her lashes at her brother and secretly stroked the hem of his coat as it lay on the pew beside her. How fortunate she would have Araminta with her as they walked out along the winding yew-shaded path through the churchyard. Last night she had dreamed that she stood on that path, dressed in mourning, beside a recent grave. She was trying to read the name carved on the stone, but as she stepped forward to read it the stone seemed to move back, out of focus, as the letters pulsed and glowed gold before her in unrecognisable characters. Now the rector was talking about "a recent melancholy event". She would not listen, with an effort she stirred herself to one of her accustomed sermontide pastimes, looking at those of the congregation she could see from her seat, deciding how she would have dressed had she been the stout beribboned woman she could see across the aisle, or her anaemic daughter so ill-served by her pale grey.

Araminta gazed up into the roof, watching the specks of dust in the sunbeam. She was disappointed there was no stained glass, but the roof was a veritable forest of timbers. She imagined it inhabited by a chattering troupe of monkeys, just like the organ grinder's little monkeys except they wore no clothes and held out no tin cup. They would look happier too, clambering around at their own pleasure. Wasn't there once a saint who preached to animals? He would have stood in the pulpit and urged the furry little creatures to remember their creator, and they would have swung from the beams by their tails and scampered away, or pelted him with nutshells. She should not be thinking like this, in such a solemn place, and with such trouble, she had for a moment forgotten. This death, shocking though it was, could not touch her like that of her little brother Samuel five years before. She wondered what the dead man's mother had hoped for him when he was Samuel's age. Perhaps it had been better to die so tenderly loved than to be killed in your old age and mourned by none. She was quite sure he had been killed. She had seen him again and again, his head, arms and chest clear in the moonlight; the rest in the shadows cast by the pillars. The cup in one hand – the lips twisted back, the eyes staring, and the other hand, palm upward, fingers drawn into a half-clenched fist. That was odd, the cup was on its side, but there was no trace of dampness trickling from it. Was that why she was so certain he had not died by his own hand? She hoped they would find everything out very soon. She had told Celestine in the darkness of the night about the figure she thought she had seen; they both agreed she must have imagined it in her highly-wrought state. "The wicked flee" the psalmist had said, "where no man pursueth" and that was what she had done. She should not have been there and so she had been frightened and run away from nothing. But a spirit, also, was "no man." She turned her attention towards the sermon with determination.

"As the Apostle James teaches us in the third chapter of his Epistle, the tongue is a tiny member but capable of great evil. Let me remind you, my good people, of the troubles that can be caused by an unbridled tongue. When a melancholy and unusual event occurs, there are always those willing to put upon that event an uncharitable and exaggerated interpretation. If I may instance; it would be greatly irresponsible and meriting the most severe punishment by the justice of God and man if any were to use the occasion of the death of a solitary recluse as an opportunity for wild speculation and lurid recrimination. Rumour is painted, as the immortal Swan of Avon reminds us, as "full of tongues", and in another place, one of his noblest characters pronounces in words that ring down the centuries:

"Who steals my purse, steals trash…

But he who filches from me my good name

Robs me of that which not enriches him

And makes me poor indeed."

And I earnestly desire to echo those profound sentiments: beware lest by idle gossip you in any way diminish the good name of your fellow-man; and in particular those who are set in temporal authority over you. Beware of malice. Resist all temptation to calumny prompted by vulgar envy…."

Were people going to talk about them like that then? Was it possible that anyone could even imagine that anyone connected with Laetitia's family might -no, it was too absurd. The rector was supposed to be very learned, but he was an old man, and like all old people was confused by strange events. He could not understand human nature as clearly as a younger man would. What a ridiculous idea!

But more than one of the congregation took to heart the rector's warning of the dangers of unbridled speech, and resolved that no slip of the tongue should reveal the guilt of the heart.

Betty's family lived on a smallholding tucked into a dip in the hills of Nidderdale. In the neat stone house lived her parents, her mother's mother, two brothers older than she was, and three younger children, two girls and a boy. The older boys, Joseph and Aaron, worked in the lead mines. Her father and mother looked after the smallholding, Mrs Grainger also doing some spinning which was collected and paid for monthly. One of her daughters helped her, while the two youngest went to the village school. Just over a year before, at the age of fifteen, Betty had left to work in the kitchen at Skells, at the suggestion of an aunt of hers who was one of the cooks, and promised to see to it that she found her way about.

Betty had at first greatly enjoyed the experience, especially the chance to see how people in other places lived. She had been fascinated to see what Lord and Lady Fenborough whom she had only seen in a carriage rushing along the high road before had for their meals. Later, as she progressed to laundry work, the delicacy and beauty of her Ladyship's garments had filled her with astonishment and admiration. She had liked to feel that she was necessary – she and the likes of her – to the exciting and interesting life she was allowed to glimpse, and was heartily glad that her father had overcome his doubts as to her safety sufficiently to allow her to gain this experience. She had not realised he had never been thoroughly reconciled to her going, and it was only the difficulty of feeding so many that had forced him to allow it. When John had burst in excitedly and begged them to send for her, hinting that all might not be well, they were seriously troubled, and determined to make room for her. Besides, Joseph and Aaron were doing well at the mine, which made life a little easier for them all.

Mrs Grainger had looked up anxiously when John brought back her daughter the day before, but neither then nor since had she seen anything in her appearance or manner to suggest she had in any way brought shame on herself and the family, and John's manner had further reassured her. It was clear that he had hopes of some day making her his bride, and the open cheerfulness of his manner as he had shared their midday meal completed her reassurance. She was now free to enjoy Betty's stories about the strange ways of the rich people she had been serving, and to laugh with her at the thought that a grown man or woman, having health of mind and body, should need to call for another to help them prepare for bed, or rise in the morning.

"Though indeed, Mother," she had laughed, "Some of the ladies are so squeezed and tight-laced that it is a wonder they can move at all, and if their friends were to see them as we do, on first waking, before we have set to work on them, they would not be able to recognise them."

"I am afraid you will find it dull here again, my child. We look the same all day long, and there is no need to spend half the day choosing among our garments! Yet I would not change with any; I pray that you and all my children may be as fortunate in home and family as I am. I do not see that her Ladyship herself could be more contented."

"No, much less so, for another strange thing about these wealthy people is that, having no real troubles, they must needs invent them. I have seen a young lady put out for a week because one was wearing a finer gown than she was at a ball where they all looked as beautiful as queens, and others take to their beds with a supposed head-ache entirely to plague and vex their husbands. You need not be troubled, Mother, they and their servants have a life I am glad to know about, but I would not wish mine to be of such a kind. One honest man, miner or carter though he be, is more to my mind than silken fops who spend their nights drinking, gaming and wenching, and never putting in a honest day's work the whole of their lives."

While they were busying themselves with the milking Betty had asked how her grandmother was, for she did not care to speak openly in the house, with the old woman dozing on the bed which had been bought for warmth into a corner of the kitchen.

"She is losing her strength; I think she is too tired to carry on with her life much further. I do not expect her to see Christmas, though I may be wrong. She is as alert and watchful as ever, and I know she is very glad to have you home. For some reason she has taken against your working at the great house, but will not tell us why. You must be patient with her, and remember that old people have their fancies."

Betty thought about her mother's words as she sat beside the fire on Sunday evening, watching the old woman as the firelight flickered on her worn hands and face. Stools and a bench had been brought in from the dairy for every Sunday night a group of the neighbours met together at the Graingers' to study the scriptures and hold fellowship with one another.

Already John had arrived, with his Uncle Marmaduke, who was clutching a well-worn Bible. Half a dozen others soon joined them, each one greeting Betty and trying to find out, some with more tact than others, why she was back home. Mrs Grainger tried to put an end to all their speculations. "I need her help with Mother and the spinning, after all she can't expect to spend her whole life among great houses."

Gradually the meeting settled, everyone was warmed and ready to leave gossip for a while. As Mr Grainger was taking up the Bible and lighting the candle beside his seat, two late arrivals came, a young farmer and his wife from several miles away. They too looked at Betty with surprise, and turning to her mother the man said, "You have moved fast to bring her away! Surely you do not think there is any danger to her from the strange doings of yesterday?"

"Whatever do you mean? What strange doings?" cried Betty, wondering whether she was the subject of unkind gossip.

"Did she not tell you? I heard of it at church this morning-leastways, after church. The rector had not much to give but dark hints, but the second groom was readier with his tongue. One of the servants has been found," the farmer paused to savour the dramatic pronouncement, " stiff and stark, with his throat cut from ear to ear!"

All eyes turned on Betty. "Why did you not tell us this before, Child,?" demanded her father.

"But – this is the very first I have heard of this. Are you sure you are not mistaken? When did it happen? Was it one of those who worked with me, and-"

"He was, it seems, found yesterday morning, in one of those godless buildings in the grounds, it has some blasphemous name which I forget."

"Would it be the Temple of Piety?"

"I think so. As if any man could properly build a temple to any other than the living God! Yes, that was the name. It was an old man, the one they called the Druid. You recall his Lordship's foolery, building a ring of stones then hiring a man to pretend he was a heathen priest."

"It's no more then than he deserved… Thou shall not take the name of the Lord thy God in vain," Uncle Marmaduke stated firmly. "It's a judgement on him and his blasphemous ways."

"I have not your confidence, I must own. And I believe the constable will not be content to leave it at that. 'Tis not God, but man, that cuts a man's throat privily by night."

"Was that when they think it was done? Now then , when did they discover the body?" Betty wanted to know.

"Early yesterday morning, one of the menservants was exercising a horse and they saw the body as they passed the temple. They brought it into the shed and sent for the surgeon, and when he came at last he said the man had been dead by the middle of the night. So, young Betty, if so be you know of anybody who wasn't where they should have been that night, your duty's clear enough. You are very well out of that sink of iniquity, in my opinion." The farmer leaned back in his chair, hands spread on his knees, well pleased with the interest he had aroused.

Mrs Grainger was alarmed by Betty's sudden pallor. She stood up and leaned over her, sheltering her face from the neighbours' kindly but curious eyes.

"You should be ashamed of yourself, Martin Horner, to speak to a young girl in that way. You have given her a terrible shock. To come blurting out with news that shows she could have been murdered in her bed – thank God you brought her away when you did John if there is some evil person lurking there – and then to suggest she might have seen or heard something at a time when all good Christians were asleep in bed. I'm sure you were well asleep by the middle of the night, were you not?"

"Yes, of course I was." And this was true. Please God, let her ask nothing more.

"There you are. Joseph, it is high time we turned to the scriptures. This is no talk for the Sabbath evening."

Betty was reassured to hear her father's voice reading as she had so often heard it before, but was unable to take any comfort from the holy words. What should she do? The ways of the gentry were strange indeed, but surely the young friend of Miss Laetitia's could have naught to do with cutting throats. And yet she had been out that night. She must think very carefully before she spoke. If only she could tell someone, but once she spoke to anyone she could no longer hide what she knew, and she did not wish to stir up trouble for any innocent person. It is impossible to take back a word once it has been spoken.

Gradually she realised what passage her father was reading, it was the one where St James tells us not to do damage with our tongues, because it can be like lighting a fire that we cannot control. So that was the answer, to keep quiet! Never before had the Scripture spoken so direct to her. Truly it must be the word of God, for who else could answer her secret thought! She could now listen to the solemn words with a sense of peace. She looked across at John and smiled at him.

Then as usual, they moved to prayer. As always, one of

the number was suggesting what they should be praying about.

"And as we pray tonight, we must remember those who are in any way afflicted by the death of the man Martin spoke about, and in my opinion we can also pray that all is well with him now he has met his Maker as we all must."

Heads were bowed in silence, broken as one of the older men, looked up, and began to say, very softly, "Brothers and sisters, tonight for the first time since we began to meet I cannot join in with your prayers. I cannot lie to God, and He knows only too well the thoughts of my heart concerning this man. I have a burden upon me to tell you all. Friends, when I first knew of this man's death my soul leapt within me, and I could not but rejoice with my whole heart.

Many years ago, when my first wife was alive, she and her little baby were desperately sick and weak. We lived in a place where we knew no-one, and I had neither food nor money in the house. The babe was crying for hunger, and my wife too weak to tend it, and near death herself. I went out desperate to find something for them and I did. Some woman had left a jug of milk and a loaf on a window sill, I took them. The next day I found work and was in want no longer. But that man, that bad man, came to my house a week later and told me he had seen me take the food. He said if I did not pay him a shilling every month he would tell the constable, and I would be transported. For two years I paid him, and at last, when money was scarce, I told him I could pay no longer, and if he must lay his information I could not prevent him. Then he told me that on the same day as I took the milk, a lamb was taken from the same farm, and he would lay information against me on that as well. I swore before God that I was innocent of that – as indeed my friends I was, and will say so to God himself on the Day of Judgement – and he laughed and asked who would believe me. God forgive me, I have given him one shilling a month from that day to this. Can you wonder that my heart is as light as a feather at his death?"

After a long silence, John said, "There is none here to blame you for that, and as for the theft so long ago, surely that is forgiven by God, if indeed it needs forgiveness, for we are given our families to provide for, and do not forget that David stole the holy bread to feed his followers, and the Lord himself said it was right for him to do so."

The farmer's wife looked up. "I doubt if it is right for justice to question his death, which well be a true blessing to many. For there was a young woman who lived in the cottage next to my parents. She has been many years dead, so I can tell you her story. She was about five years older than me, and when I was ten she went away to work. A few months later she came back and child that I was I could see she had lost her peace of mind. She went for long walks alone. She had been accustomed to sing at her work, but now span silently, with a sad face. Much later she told that she had found out that she was with child and desperate lest her parents discovered her guilt and turned her away from her home, she had taken a draught to make her miscarry. She had buried the still-born infant beneath an oak tree in the woods behind the village, and thought nobody knew what she had done. One evening, as she was walking that way, as she often did, this man we have been talking of stepped forward from behind the oak. He told her he had been watching her, and knew what was buried at the tree roots. Unless she gave him five shillings that month, and every year thereafter on the same date, he would share his knowledge with the whole village. Every year she found the money for him, and when she married, five years later, he increased the sum to ten shillings, for he knew her husband was a man of violent temper and easily roused. She had not been married a twelvemonth when she took sick of a fever and died. My mother nursed her, and told me she need not have died, but seemed without the will to recover her strength. I believe she was glad to die, because it was only death which could release her from her perpetual fear. And so I, too, am glad he is gone, and see the hand of God in the killing of such a wicked man."

There was some murmuring at this. "We are told," said Uncle Marmaduke, "that the civil authorities are to be obeyed, and they require us to help bring criminals to their just reward. To kill any privily is against the laws of God and man, and may by no means be ignored."

"Indeed, the miscreant must be laid by the heels; but I would not wish to think it was by my information."

There was variety of opinion among the group in the kitchen, but no doubt within Betty herself. To think she had made this man comfortable in the kitchen, and helped him to mulled ale. She had felt pity for his lonely life, and the way so many of her fellow servants avoided speaking to him, and slipped out of the kitchen shortly after he crossed the threshold.

First one, then another, made their petitions for their own and the life of the dale. Betty's prayer was silent and fervent, " Help me, O Lord, to keep my wits about me, and avoid any traps that might be set by the constable, and let no careless word of mine bring trouble on any poor sinner who has brought his torment to an end by the death of this wicked, wicked man." For now, even if she had seen the killing herself, she would not lift a finger to catch the murderer.

Monday October 18th

My dear Louisa,

I shall not harrow your spirits by alluding in this letter to the melancholy news I wrote to our parents, except to tell you that, having by now recovered from the alarm and unpleasantness occasioned by that unexpected death, I do hope to be allowed to remain here for the period originally proposed at the outset of my visit. For a while I was deeply affected. I thought feelingly of our own great loss a few years ago; and I was also troubled for another reason which I will tell you when I see you. Now I must own that my wish to remain is not unconnected with some far more pleasant intelligence received this morning.

Letty and I were in the drawing room after breakfast. She was in low spirits, and in order to provide us both with amusement, I suggested we should try to persuade her little dog, Laura, to pose for her portrait. We would each endeavour to draw her as best we could, and Celestine would judge whose was the best effort. Was this not generous of me? Letty has always drawn rather better than I, and even were this not so, Celestine could hardly prefer my work to hers, out of common courtesy.. Letty agreed, and while I sharpened our pencils she brushed Laura's coat until it shone and sent her maid to fetch a bunch of ribbons. Then we had to decide what colour and shape of bow would suit Laura best. The poor creature sat very patiently while we tried green, red, blue and striped ribbons in various sizes. Had I been so mauled about and pestered, and possessed of her sharp little teeth, I do not think my tormentors would have escaped unscathed, but apart from growling a little when we pulled her hair, she stayed contentedly on the cushion on which we placed her..

But when we tried to surround the cushion with a trail of ivy leaves we had gathered from outside the window she could endure it no longer. With a loud yapping she leapt upon the stem, and shook and worried it until all the leaves lay about in fragments while she dashed around the room, dragging the main stem with her, with us in hot pursuit, fearful lest she run into and upset one of the dainty little tables and bring its precious ornaments to the carpet with a crash! At last she wearied of her game, dropped the stem, trotted back to the cushion and reclined upon it, quiescent. She did indeed present a charming sight, with a blue satin bow atop her head and her little pink tongue quivering. I regretted the fate of the ivy; not only because picking up the fragments was a tedious task, but the more because I can draw very tasteful wreaths of ivy. I decided to surround my picture with an imaginary garland of holly and ivy.

Finally we settled to work. The bows we drew were a joy to behold; Miss Browne, our drawing mistress in York, taught us all how to draw ribbons exceedingly well, but Laura herself was far more difficult of execution. She would keep breathing, and turning her head away, or twitching one paw – always the paw one was at that moment trying to represent. We were engrossed in our work for a long time, until about twelve o'clock. I could not get the front paws right, and was just beginning to add a few extra leaves to the wreath to conceal them when the door opened and Lord Fenborough came in.

He smiled at us, and said he was pleased to see us so constructively occupied. We explained we were sketching in competition, and invited him to judge between us, which he declined – to my regret, for had he done so, he must have found for me, He then - and here is the news – went on, " I am so glad to see you both in good spirits, for I feared you might be downcast. Laetitia, my dear, it is some time since we had any dancing here, not since last winter. Would you and your friend like us to hold an informal ball here on Friday night, for a number of our friends and neighbours?"

Well, I ask you, Louisa, would we? I have not danced this twelvemonth. And while I was struggling to find words to express my delight and astonishment, he had yet more to unfold to us. "Lady Fenborough is intending to go to Harrogate tomorrow to take the waters. How would you both like to accompany her and amuse yourselves in the town, while she is at the Spa. It will be a chance to purchase ribbons and trinkets – and material for a new gown if you would like one."

Even while I was regretting that it would not be possible for me to ask father for a new gown I was making a suitably grateful reply. Letty only smiled at him, and grew pink with pleasure. He chucked her under the chin saying, "Well, mouse, this is better than sitting and moping is it not?" Then, as he turned to go: "Your mother needs you this afternoon; she wishes you to read to her. Araminta, if you wish to walk or ride with your maid in the grounds today, I would like you to take one of the men servants with you. I am sure there can be no danger, but his presence will give both reassurance and protection."

He was gone, and Letty with shining eyes, turned to me, and said, "This must be for your sake. I have not known him so playful for a long time. Now, what do you think I should look my best in?" I tried to enter into her plans with enthusiasm, but could not but regret that I had only a little money with me, enough only for the ribbons and trinkets Lord Fenborough had mentioned. But later, when I told Celestine all about it, she said that Papa had given her £10 before we left, "in case she would want a new gown. I do not want my daughter to feel herself less well turned out than her friend." And she says that if I bring the material home tomorrow, and do not plague her to do a hundred other things, she will be able to have it made by Friday! I think perhaps I would like a daffodil colour, maybe with a small print, or perhaps a pale blue, like Laura's bow. Not pink, my last was pink and I feel now it has rather a childish look. And I will be able to choose the material all by myself, with Laetitia for company and to help me make up my mind, but not to tell me what I may not have. Celestine has drawn me a picture of what it will look like, and is working out for me how much material I will have to buy.

Laetitia expects there to be about a dozen couple, which should give us a pleasantly crowded room. I only hope the gentlemen (or at least the young, handsome ones) will not prefer to spend all their time playing cards, as I have heard they sometimes do. How terrible it would be to lack a partner, especially when everyone else was standing up. I would never recover from the humiliation. But surely this will not happen. It is to be Lord Fenborough's ball, and in his house, so a young lady actually of his party cannot be ignored. Besides, I can own to you only, that I do not think I will look such a fright as to deserve neglect. Four days to wait! Friday will never come – but when I said the same to Celestine she reminded me that she would need the time if my gown is to be ready in all its glory.

This afternoon, she and I went for a ride in the park. One of the men went with us as Lord Fenborough had arranged. He was armed with a pistol! Although it is no doubt the height of romance to be protected by an armed escort, I will own it made me a little uncomfortable, even though he assured us he was skilled in handling firearms. I was most relieved he had no occasion to demonstrate his prowess. We did not however ride far, though far enough for your timorous sister who saw lurking villains beneath every tree. We kept well away from the scene of the recent sad events, you may be sure.

I will enclose a copy of Celestine's sketch for the new gown. She is going to dress my hair as she has drawn in the picture.
I hope you have opportunity to dance soon, too.
My dearest love to all of you.
Araminta

* * *

The ride that afternoon had been of more interest than Araminta intended her sister to realise. When their horses were led up to them they found that their escort was to be

Porrott, a circumstance which at first made Araminta feel a little uneasy. Celestine, when she saw the pistol, asked him if he thought he could disable a miscreant with it, and he replied that he was not unfamiliar with the use of firearms, and that was why Lord Fenborough had detailed this task to him.

They rode away from the lake, through the deer park. Araminta reined in her horse to look at a distant group of animals under the trees, trying to count them with difficulty as they wandered among the dead leaves nibbling the thin grass. She turned to see Porrott and Celestine deep in conversation. Alarmed, she rejoined them, crying, "What is amiss? What is it that you are discussing so earnestly? Have you seen anything strange?"

Celestine replied, "Porrott was the inquest this morning, miss, and was telling me about it. I did not know if you would care to hear."

"Oh but I do. What did they bring in? Do they think he killed himself?"

"They decided there was not sufficient evidence to show how he met his death. The surgeon who opened the body was called - but you will not wish to hear details of his evidence."

"No. Indeed!"

"It seemed to me that the coroner would gladly have had a verdict of felo de se, and he leaned hard on the jury to decide it that way, laying great stress on the yew berries, but they –"

"Yew berries? What about them?"

"It was said the dead man's mouth was full of them, and he held a bunch of them clenched tightly in his right hand."

After a moment of silent amazement, Celestine said quietly, "But I thought –"

" Yes, I know. You are right. When we saw the body in the middle of the night there was nothing in his hand. The berries were there when I found him in the morning. Someone must have put them there after we had gone away, and that is how we three know he did not kill himself. Celestine, and Miss Araminta, we must let nobody know that we know this. I am very glad of this opportunity to speak with you both. Has either of you told anybody of our adventures of that night?"

Both assured him that they had not. "I am heartily glad to hear it," he went on, "for if anyone else should discover that we saw the body as we did, I fear our own lives would be in danger. Now, Miss, keep a hold of yourself, we can't have you fainting every time you go out. So long as you keep mum you are safe enough."

"But, " asked Celestine sharply, "when were the berries put in position? You say they were there when you found the body in the morning. Is that why you looked so pale and troubled as you rode into the yard?"

"It was indeed. I knew by the berries that the man had been murdered, and an attempt made to ensure the inquest would find he killed himself. Yet I dare not speak of what I knew - for the sake of all of us."

"What….. what about the cup?" Araminta recalled her persistent vision, "Nothing had spilled from it onto the ground. Was it…."

"Do you not think it means he was not killed there, but brought to the spot dead, and set in the Temple of Piety as if on a stage?"

"And in that case," Celestine's voice trembled as she spoke, "we might have almost interrupted the murderer at his work. I wonder if he could have been watching the whole time."

"I think it is much more likely that he – or they – would take fright when he first realised someone else was in the grounds, and would run away, returning much later. For indeed, had anyone been there so near as to risk capture, would he not have…."

They all left the sentence unfinished. A murderer disturbed in his scene setting would be more likely to strike again, and at once, than to await developments. Why not kill again, two, three or four times, once murder had been committed?

Porrott continued, "As I said, I do not think it at all likely that we have been recognised, and you are surely safe enough within the house, with friends and servants within call at all times, But I wonder if you would not be better at home, both of you."

"I am not sure," Celestine replied. "We must do nothing to arouse suspicion, and I think it would be too unexpected for my young lady to go home when a ball is in question on Friday."

"Indeed I will not go home. What, and miss such excitement!" Araminta felt brave enough in broad daylight. "Besides, I want to stay for Letty's sake. And there is another thing, too." She added in a low voice. " If I run away now, I shall never be able to forget, or to know what really did happen."

"And you feel you want to know that? "

"I must know, I must.. Perhaps the Constable will be able to discover-"

"I intend to make it my business to find out the truth. Providence guided me to the place where we found this body, and with the help of Providence I intend to see that justice is done and the truth established."

Porrott's fine words carried the force of a vow. Both young women were troubled by his solemnity.

Araminta shivered in the sudden breeze and turned her mount. "Let us ride on for a while, it is becoming cold. I do not want to stay out too long."

After Celestine had seen her mistress into the company of the other ladies for tea she sought out Porrott. "Do act with caution if you intend to seek out the guilty party. I would be sorry for you to run into danger."

"I will indeed be careful. I have no wish to be found in the same case as the poor druid."

"But once you start asking questions you will be noticed, and then..."

"There may indeed be some slight risk. But what of that? I am young and strong, and bored with a petty life of obsequiousness and service. It will at least be interesting, and if it is dangerous – well, I am a single man with no family or friends to grieve if disaster overtakes me."

"Do not be too sure of that; I at least would be sorry for any man to be destroyed by his courage. But now, if you are determined to find out what you can, I had better tell you all I know about that evening."

She explained where Araminta had gone first, and about the light she said she had seen. She did not mention the apparition of the monk, being by no means certain her mistress had actually seen any such figure. She did not ask Porrott why he had been abroad, but after a moment he said:

"You must wonder what I was doing out at that time. I was looking out of my window, and thought I saw a light where there should be none, so I set out to discover its source, but I saw nothing out of the ordinary until I met you both."

"Can you tell me what the surgeon said? You were right not to tell her, but I would like to know – and indeed, she may ask from me what she would not hear from you."

"He said the appearance of the corpse was such that he could not be satisfied that he died of yew poisoning. The face had the appearance of one who had been stifled, although he could not discount the possibility that the deceased had choked on the berries rather than been poisoned by them. I do not know why, but the coroner was certainly mighty anxious that a verdict of suicide should be brought in."

"I do not suppose that Lord Fenborough would be grateful to any official that caused there to be a manhunt upon his land. Will you tell us what you propose to do next?"

"When I leave you I will find opportunity to search the stone circle, and particularly the Druid's cave."

"And will you tell me – us – what you find there? And there is something else I would like you to do for us. Can you ensure that it is you who takes the ladies to Harrogate tomorrow, and can you make sure that the horse casts a shoe so that they will not be back before evening? That is, if you do not remain overnight, as I think you may do. I have a little private business I would transact tomorrow."

"Do not go near the circle or the cave, I beg you."

"And what is it to you , sir, where I go or do not go? But I will not go there, and I shall take care of myself. After all, I have a ball gown to make between tomorrow and Friday, and my young mistress will die of chagrin if any interfering murderer prevents my accomplishing the task!"

Tuesday October 19th

The rector, gazing absently out of his study window, watched the liveried coach roll along the road in the grey drizzle. It was the only event of any interest which had occurred that morning. As usual at this time, he was at his desk writing.

When he had set out on his project many months before he had seen clearly a title page in his mind's eye:

The Psalms of David

Newly Done into English, Amplified and Improved

According to the most Elegant Canons of Taste

Of the Best Cricticks

Both Ancient and Modern

By the Revd Septimus Maltravers A.M.

The Hebrew Bible, to feature so prominently in the portrait that would provide the engraving to face this title page was behind him on the bookshelves that lined the walls. On the desk were the *Book of Common Prayer*, the *King James Bible*, and the *Essay on Criticism* by Alexander Pope who, despite his outlandish name and religion, had been a most accomplished poetical writer. Today he was dealing with the eighth psalm, for he was not following any set pattern in his work. "O Lord our Lord, how excellent is Thy name in all the earth!" Stirring words, and admirable sentiments, but a trifle unpolished for this elegant age. He dipped his pen in the inkwell and began:

Great Lord our God! The welkin doth proclaim

With one accord the glories of Thy name.

For naught that lives, how'er it lowly be

Withholds at all Thy rightful Praise from Thee.

Each infant frail upon its mother's breast…

rest? best? West? Temporarily defeated, as so many composers of couplets have been, by the relative paucity of rhyming words in English, the rector laid down his pen and leaned back in his chair.

The room was more imposing than pleasant. A warm fire blazed in the grate, flickering on the dark red and green tiles of the fireplace. The panelling was a rather darker shade than he liked, but there was no denying its quality and it certainly gave an effect of solemnity to the room entirely in keeping with his position in the community. The windows, with crimson curtains, were large, but as they faced north the room was seldom seen in sunlight. From his reclined position he could no longer see the road or his garden, only the tops of the churchyard yews against the grey sky. He watched them swaying in the gusts of wind, and saw by consulting his watch that in less than half an hour the bell would summon him to the dining room, where he and Lydia would sit at each end of the oak table, being served an excellent meal by well-trained servants. She would ask him how his work had progressed; he would reply politely and enquire after her concerns of the morning. Nothing of moment had ever transpired. Was there not a text somewhere about "a dinner of herbs, where love is" being preferable to a feast without it?

He looked again at the yew trees and the grey sky. How different from the dark cypresses against the rich blue skies of Italy. How often had he sat, gazing out from a far humbler room, lazily watching them brushing against the pure blue – a blue he had felt (for had been a young man then) to be almost a holy colour.

His father had sent him abroad to travel after the university. The third son, he was destined for the church, but his father had wished him to see something of the world as a gentleman should before taking orders and settling into one of the livings he was confident he could persuade one of his noble friends to provide.

So that summer, he and the servant had come to Umbria, and stayed for a few nights in the village inn of San Marcellino. He had not then found the place beautiful but stifling, sticky and lice-infested. The day before they were due to leave he had fallen sick of a fever, and the servant, fearful of infection, had fled, taking with him the greater part of their stock of money and clothing. He knew nothing of this at the time; for days he was aware only of heat, weakness and pain. Later he had lain still, drifting in and out of dreams, sliding into sleep with no sense of volition, recognising at times gentle, competent hands and a comforting voice.

In his convalescence he lay at peace in a small, clean bed in a whitewashed room, watching the shafts of sunlight from the high window move across the uneven wall and recognised in Maria, the daughter of the house, the hands and voice that had comforted him. He watched her too, as she fed him broth and tended the room. His recovery was gradual and happy; in that poor room with only the girl to attend him he grew in peace and confidence.

One warm day as he was sitting in the parlour of the inn, waiting for his meal he thought he would soon be able to leave. In a few days he could buy himself a horse, ride off down the valley, and leave this quiet little village behind. Then Maria came in with the bread and soup. He watched her set the tray on the table, and the shape of her arm and the curve of her neck were the most beautiful things in the world. He could not leave them. He told her that he was now almost well, and the swift look she gave him before composing her face to cheerful encouragement told him she had no wish for him to depart. Strange, he had read so much about the phenomenon of love, but its presence filled him with shocked delight. All was perfect; he stayed.

But Maria was a good daughter of the church and had three older brothers. She and her family were eager for a wedding; she for love and trust; they for fear of treachery on his part. But could they not see it was impossible? Could he take her away from family and lifetime friends, back to the chilly splendours of his father's estate? Nothing could be done.... But the days drifted by, full of summer scents and drowsy mirages and somehow he found himself in the dark little church before an old priest, exchanging vows of eternal fidelity with her... it could not be a real church, this den of superstition, nor could it be a real marriage, but she was made very happy by it, and perhaps all would be well after all.

For a while he too was happy, as never before or since. He came to love every detail of their simple life because he shared it with her. Little Maria was born a year after the marriage. She had her mother's dark eyes and his fair hair and she was beautiful. He wondered at her tiny, strong fingers and clenched toes, and when he watched Maria suckle the child he knew more reverence than before any of the splendid portrayals of the Virgin and Child he had dutifully paraded before in Florence. And yet, and yet... It must be an interlude, He could not bring it to an end, but it could not last for ever. He could not grow grey and portly as a village innkeeper.

She was pregnant again, and in his secret heart he thought it would be terribly sad but somehow fitting if she were to die in childbed – but it was the child, his only son, who died, and Maria recovered. Little Maria was now walking and beginning to chatter and at times he thought he saw in her the hint of a coarseness of feature and gesture inherited from her grandmother. He was very gentle towards Maria who was a long time recovering her strength.

Then the letter came. His father had made enquiries when he had not come home at the time expected and traced the recreant servant. He, eager to avert any suspicion that he might have done away with his young master, had told him about the sickness at the inn, and his father wrote there in an attempt to discover where he now was. In the letter he summoned him home as soon as possible; "You have been travelling long enough, and it is high time you settled down. I have arranged that you should be presented with the living of Stokeley Reall this Autumn. It is also time to think about marriage." He told his son that he desired him to pay court to the daughter and only child of a neighbouring landowner; both fathers were eager for the match, the lady was presumed to be willing, all that was needed for a satisfactory conclusion was his presence and agreement. He sent him sufficient money to travel home in an appropriate manner, as he feared his prolonged silence might in part be due to financial embarrassment.

When he received the letter he went for a long walk. It never occurred to him to disobey the summons; he knew his duty. But he resolved never again to allow himself to care so much for another human creature. She is becoming possessive, he told himself fiercely. I never liked her mother and her father drinks far too much. I was beginning to feel disgusted and bored by her ignorance. Better it should end like this than in bickering and pettiness. I am grateful to her, she has been good to me according to her ability, but this must be the end.

He went to see the priest and told him that his father had written, insisting on his immediate return. Filial obedience could not be denied. He hinted his father was aged and infirm (infirm indeed! He rode to hounds thrice a week) and wished to see him before he died. The priest was sympathetic. "How long do you think you will have to be gone? I am glad you have a wife and child to take to cheer his old age. It will not be easy for Maria to leave her family, but you would have to return to your father sometime, and I am sure she will do her best in a strange land, love your father and tend him as she should."

Guilt fuelled indignation. Did the old fool actually think that the mumbo-jumbo he had conducted was a real wedding? Did he not understand that one of his station did not wed an innkeeper's daughter? He explained that, for various reasons, including Maria's continuing weakness, it would not be possible to take her and the child with him this time. He hoped to return soon, and in the meantime Maria must write often.

"But how can she? I am the only person in the village who can read or write. You will have to send to me for news of her, and to tell us of your return. If you have to be away a long time it would only be right for you to send some money, for as you know, the family is not wealthy."

He had promised. Two days later – days which he so firmly refused to recall that he had at last forgotten them – he set out for home in a daze of guilt and sentimental regret. He had promised to return within a few months. Maria he thought had believed him. Her mother had not.

His father was pleased to see him home and had lost little time in bringing about a meeting with his prospective bride. She was handsome enough and with a well formed figure fashionably dressed. He obliged his father with less difficulty than he had expected. There was so little comparison between the two women in person, character or situation, such discontinuity between the two marriages that he had little sense of infidelity. He felt rather as if two young men, resident in his body, had each taken a wife. He wrote occasionally to Maria via the priest and sent money to support the child. The letters that the priest wrote were at first full of news of little Maria, and looked confidently forward to his return. Later they became more restrained and finally resigned to his protracted absence. Maria never knew of his second marriage.

Ten years ago came the last letter from the priest. Maria had died of a fever similar to that through which she had nursed him and young Maria, now fifteen, was being cared for by the nuns. Had he any further wishes with regard to her, or would he entrust her future to the good nuns? He added that Maria had always hoped for his return, and had always loved her English husband faithfully.

He had been disturbed when the letter came – he was indignant that his only child could be placed in a convent, and sorry for poor faithful Maria – but far more disturbed when he had discovered that it was missing from the inner drawer where he had placed it.

Three years it was since the terrible discovery. Lydia surely could not have taken it. She was incapable of keeping to herself the minutest detail which gave legitimate grounds for complaint. He had scrutinised the servants carefully, but in no eyes could he detect the look that surely must be there if they had read the letter. He had not dared to dismiss any of then since he had discovered his loss. Lydia was often irritated by his unexacting attitude.

Then six months after the letter was taken, he had ridden to the fair at Pateley Bridge. While he was picking his way through the main street a beggar pushed through the crowd and clung to his stirrup. Angrily he told the man to go away.

The beggar did not move, but took a firmer grip, and asked for alms in a loud, whining voice. "For the love of God sir, some pence for bread. By all the saints, for the sake of Maria di San Marcellino, food for a poor sinner with a wife and daughter to support!" He had started and given the man the first coin he found, a half sovereign, and the man had melted away as quickly as he had come. And every three months or so he had met the beggar again, who accosted him with the same words, and received the same reward. Terrible though this persecution was, there was comfort in the thought that the man would not readily lose a good source of income for the sake of blind malice. A month ago, he thought he had pierced the disguise and recognised the man. And if he was right the man was dead.

But what of the letter? Had anyone had the chance to search his belongings and find the letter in its hiding place? And would he or she be more interested in a regular income or in causing scandal? Little wonder that the rector could not with ease concentrate on composing his couplets.

He had no guilt towards God for what he had done, for God had always been to him a proposition only, and no shame within himself; obedience to parents was a paramount duty and besides, it would have been the merest superstition to consider the priest's ceremony as binding upon an English Protestant. But he thought he could barely endure the shame of Lydia discovering the secret of his low affections in early life. He cringed inwardly when he imagined its becoming known among his congregation. The shame to him, and to his church, and to his whole family! The villages around were teeming with rabid enthusiasts, always watching him and measuring him. They would show no mercy to him or the church. No, he had no remorse for what he had done, but a great deal of anxiety.

The bell summoned him for lunch. Lydia was for once animated, eager to hear details of the previous day's inquest. "Had anyone any suggestions as why a person should seek to kill such a harmless, if strange, old man? I wonder if there are any gypsies about? Perhaps he caught them poaching and so they killed him."

He told her that the man had died by violence and at the hand of a person or persons unknown, told her of Lord Fenborough's indignation that the man should so humiliate his patron and pollute his grounds by his lurid death, told her of the stolid young groom's account of the discovery of the body, told her an unending coil of circumstances; while behind his eyes there beat a verse from a psalm he had not considered that morning: "Whither shall I flee from Thy presence? If I make my bed in Sheol, behold, Thou art there."

The Marquis of Granby Hotel
Harrowgate
Tuesday night

My dearest Louisa,

It is now near midnight but I am sitting up to write to you so that you can share with me in the delights and excitement of this day.

As I told you was our intent, this morning we set out for Harrowgate – Lady Fenborough, her maid Leonie, Laetitia, Celestine and I in the coach, Lord Fenbrough and two servants riding with us. I had not at first intended to bring Celestine but decided I could not well do without her. His Lordship had decided that his wife could well be fatigued after taking the waters, and recalling also that the doctors recommend that one who has done so should sleep for some hours in a warm bed, he had determined that we were all to spend the night at an hotel in the town, returning the next day. (except for Celestine: she has already ridden back with one of the grooms and is to begin on the The Gown at first light.)

It was a drizzly morning, and though the coach was both chilly and crowded with five of us inside I would not have changed with the riders, although Lord Fenborough rode a fine black horse I would fain mount on a sunny day for a ride in the woods. We passed the Rectory, grim and gloomy behind the tall yew hedge of the church yard and it seemed to me a forbidding place – how different from our own stone vicarage where we used to play with our cousins. Do you remember the day when we christened the new kittens and Tom fought Edward as to who should be the parson? I was so angry when Edward won that I would not hand over my kitten to him but christened it myself. Edward in a rage said it was not really christened because I was a girl. How proud I was when I asked my uncle if that were true and he told me that if a little baby was in grave danger of death anyone could and should christen it. I told Edward that the kitten was in danger, for George was looking for them to drown, and so I had done right! The rector here is rather old and of lofty bearing. You can see he has never had children falling out of his apple trees and riding ponies in the orchard. I am not even sure he has ever laughed!

We sped along the new turnpike road. There was a dear little girl in the window of the turnpike cottage who leaned out and showed me her doll while the toll was paid. But even so, it was a tedious journey, and we were all glad to arrive safely in Harrowgate. It had stopped raining, but the streets were sloppy. There seemed to me to be a great number of coaches and fashionable ladies, but Laetitia whispered to me that the season was almost over. I suppose that in high summer you can hardly breathe for ladies, lapdogs and liveried lackeys.

I have chosen my silk! I hardly dare to tell you – it is bright red, the colour of poppies. Would that my hair was the colour of the ripe corn in which they grow rather than the mousey brown it is! I know you will all say it is not quite the colour for a young girl, but I was determined to have it. Laetitia looks far older than I do, even though I am a month her senior. I could see Celestine was not best pleased, for she kept showing me other silks, white sprigged with flowers, and suggested we looked elsewhere. She said, which is true, that I could not wear my coral necklace with it. Then she added quietly, "It is for you to choose your own material, of course, but with many young men white is a favourite colour; I have heard her Ladyship's maid say that her son can not abide bright colours." As will guess, this brought my colour up; as if I cared for Master Frederick's preferences! "Thank you, Celestine," I replied. "That has decided me. I will have the red." She made no more ado and the silk was bought. I think Laetitia admires my decisiveness and approves my taste – I am sure she was worried that I would choose a pale blue, the same colour as hers.

When we met at the inn, Lord Fenborough had a surprise for us. We were to go to a play! The town has as yet no theatre, but plays are acted from time to time in the barn behind the hotel where we were staying. Strange as it may seem, it is no disgrace for gentlemen and ladies to watch the actors in such a place. Lord Fenborough himself escorted us, leaving his wife to Leonie, a fashionably dressed woman with pinched lips, who had no purpose in life beyond the adornment of her mistress. She affects to despise Celestine.

The play was called Macbeth. If you ever have opportunity to see it, do so. It is all about a handsome and brave soldier with a wicked wife, who turns to murder to fuel his foul ambitions, and there are witches who dance, and mislead him, and show him terrible visions, and the ghost of a friend he has killed comes before him all gory while he is sat at his royal banquet – for he becomes King – and he comes to a most horrible end. Laetitia is quite in love with Malcolm, who is the rightful King once his father has been so foully murdered, and wishes she could be his wife to comfort him in his exile, but I do not. What? Admire a man who runs away in fear after his father has been killed! I prefer Macbeth himself, for not only was he brave in battle and handsome, but not such a wicked man as he seems by his actions, for his bloodthirsty wife led him astray. I would have been a good wife and taught him to be patient and wait until the rightful king and his heir were slain in battle and then we would be King and Queen together – but then there would be no play!

Although Lady Macbeth is a terrible woman I still like her better than the wife of Macduff, who was always troubling herself about her husband's danger when he was away, and fancying herself sick, just like poor Aunt Eliza. She was staying with Lady Macbeth, and I am sure she found her a most troublesome guest. She did not deserve to be killed though. Perhaps it would be best to be Hecate, Queen of the Witches, and command the Powers of Darkness and bring about the downfall of those who trusted me too well. Lord Fenborough says the play is much altered and refined from the barbarous days when it was first writ. Oh, and Lady Macbeth runs mad with remorse and walks in her sleep and tells all her guilt. I own I was glad we had no long journey back to the comfort of our rooms.

Letty and I talked of the play while we prepared for bed. She is now asleep, and when I have sealed this letter I shall leave all the ghosts and evil powers behind, and fall asleep thinking of my new red gown.

My very dearest love to you all,
Araminta

* * *

Araminta looked up from folding her letter. She saw the candle flame reflected in the black window, and beyond it – like the apparition in the witches' cave – a pale, shadowy form. It reminded her of the face she had glimpsed in the Temple of Piety. She dared not cry out, and clasped her hand to her mouth. In horrible parody, the apparition did the same. She wrenched her head aside to see Laetitia calmly sleeping and was conscious that the vision also turned. She forced herself to stare directly at the pallid shape. After all ghosts belong to plays and nursery tales, wicked people saw them, not innocent girls. It was no supernatural visitant but her own face that she had seen. She could not now see how she had mistaken it. For all that she drew the curtains trembling and crouched by the dying fire. The face had reminded her that not only on the stage did a man or woman set out to take the life of another. Someone, perhaps someone she had met, had done that, just like Macbeth. And he perhaps knew too that she had "seen what she should not". Banquo had died for his dangerous knowledge. Was it really true that there were no witches any more? In daylight the idea was ridiculous. But at night......
Whenever she was frightened as a child she drove away her fears by reciting the multiplication tables as fast as possible. She found herself doing this again now, then, with hardly a pause for breath, racing through her evening prayer and

huddling herself into bed beside Laetitia. Her friend's steady breathing calmed her, and as she grew warmer and the candles burnt lower she thought about her lovely new gown, and how she would enter the ballroom by the great double doors. All chatter would cease for a moment as the eyes of all turned upon her, and then resume as each guest asked who she was. Before she had reached her chair she was besieged by handsome young men and Frederick had to wait a long time before she had a dance to spare for him. She was dancing with a tall young man, with flowing dark hair, who suddenly changed from a younger son in a fawn embroidered coat into a scarlet cloaked, earring wearing Barbary corsair, who whirled her down the set, out through the doors, on to his black charger, away to his vessel to the Spanish Main in search of gold, doubloons, diamonds and islands loud with red, blue and yellow birds, lofty palm trees and sun on sparkling sands.

Araminta slept. The candles burnt themselves out.

Wednesday October 20th

Celestine was riding pillion behind Porrott. They had set out much earlier, but the horse had cast a shoe and it had taken a long time to find a smith willing to work that evening. It was dark when they set out again, but the night was clear and the moon almost full. Both needed to be back at Skells the next morning, the road was good and well known to man and mount so they determined on a night journey. Celestine was glad Porrott was armed, she had no desire to be abducted by highwayman or corsair.

She was deciding how to make the gown. The neck had better be fairly high, and perhaps a chaplet of late red and white roses in her hair would emphasise her youth. She did not expect Araminta's mother either to like the gown or reproach her for allowing it. "In a few years now" she had said "Araminta may well be in charge of running a household; give her her way in anything which is not wrong or extremely foolish." The scarlet was foolish but not extremely foolish. Besides, she was consoled by her charge's reaction to the name of Frederick. She knew she had arrived with a keen interest in her friend's older brother, an interest which Celestine's own observation had led her to deplore, even before that afternoon's conversation while she and Porrott were waiting at the forge.

"Celestine, will you tell me something? Did Araminta's family send her to Skells with a view to her capturing Master Frederick?"

Indignantly she had protested that the visit was to her

friend Laetitia, that there was no need for Araminta to set out to "capture" anyone, and her parents valued happiness and security above wealth.

"I am glad of it. This master of mine has been the ruin of a number of young ladies and I have felt little pity for any of the simpering minxes. But this time – I hope you will not think me too free – she seems a happy, pleasant girl, almost too innocent for her age. I would not like to think of her or you disgraced."

Disquieted by his remark she had turned the subject to the strange death which linked the three of them together, and asked about his errand of the evening before.

"I went to the Druid's circle and cave, to see if there might be anything in his personal possessions to indicate why and at whose hand he had met his death."

"Were you observed? Did you find anything?"

"No, for someone had been there before me. There was a wooden chest with brass clasps. That had been forced open, and there was nothing inside except a few clothes, all disordered. The linings had been slit. His pots were broken, and in places the earth had been dug up. Someone had searched thoroughly, and taken away something that had been buried, making no attempt at concealment. All the little ledges and holes in the rock walls were empty, and torn moss showed that they had been searched."

"And are there any yew trees near the cave or circle?"

"There are not. There are plenty in other places, though, beside the lake and all along the walks. Anyone could have gathered them… I think he may have been stifled while abed in the cave."

"Was there a struggle?"

"I do not think so. I think the person who killed him took the body to where we found it and arranged it as we saw, and then went back to search the cave and circle. I cannot tell if he found all he sought."

Then the smith called to them that the horse was ready and they set off.

They made good time along the road in the moonlight and were not far from the turnpike cottage when Porrott drew rein suddenly. Then he quietly edged the great horse off the road into the shadows. The arms around his waist stiffened, and a cold voice in his ear whispered, "Ride on, please. I have good nails, and I always carry my scissors. Dare to lay a rough hand on me and I will-"

"Quiet, you silly girl. Listen, can you not hear?"

Celestine threw back her hood and listened. At first she heard only the thump of her own blood and the horse's breathing, then rustling sounds as small creatures stirred in the undergrowth, and a distant stream. There was no wind. Then, in the distance, a confused noise of shouting and cheering. She followed his pointing hand and saw, far in front of them on the road ahead, an unexpected light, a light which grew and wavered and grew again as she watched.

"What can it be?"

"I think it must be the turnpike cottage in flames. The lead miners hate the new road and the great tolls they are made to pay on their ore as they take it down to the port at Borrowbridge. I think a mob of them must have come together to destroy the gate and cottage. There have been riots before over the turnpikes. We must avoid the road: it would not be good to be caught by a lawless mob, particularly one which has already earned the gallows."

It was difficult to ride forward quietly, for where the trees afforded shade there were dry leaves and twigs underground. "Wait a moment." Porrott dismounted, and she could hear him at one of the saddlebags, then sense him moving round the horse, lifting one foot at a time. He remounted cautiously, and when they moved on she realised he had muffled the hooves in cloth, ."Don't worry; it's sacking, not silk." They picked their way forward, moving deeper into the wood as they neared the flame. Porrott suddenly stopped.

Peering through the branches, now dark, now edged with thin orange lines reflecting the roaring flames, they saw a swirling mass of dark shadows. They were shouting and swaying, some feeding the fire with timber. The gates had been hacked down with axes and set alight against the cottage walls. By now the thatch and all the wooden beams were alight, the fire inside leaping through the window spaces to join the freer flames outside. There was a horrible, hungry rushing sound behind the cheers and shrieks. There were too many to count in the reeling crowd, mostly men but some women – or at least, figures in women's clothes, for all wore hoods of sacking, tied at the neck, with eye slits. One huge figure in a skirt was tearing out the pages from a ledger to feed the flames. From the branch of a tree caught in the firelight something dangled and span slowly from the end of a rope.

The scene before her began to spin in time with the figure, and darkness was rushing up towards her. She felt her wrist grasped tightly and Porrott's whisper," Take hold of yourself, I beg you. 'Tis not the poor turnpike man but a pillow in his clothes. Look again and you will see 'tis but an effigy."

As she saw through her fingers that it was so, she felt her companion freeze and retreat further into the thick trees. She leaned towards him and he placed his hand over her mouth. In the firelight he had seen further than she. On the other side of the road the flames had shown up for a moment two long metal tubes pointing at the highway. Two people were lying in wait, with muskets, for any travellers. After a long minute he judged they were safe from any accident of sudden flame. The crowd had settled to raucous singing, drunk with triumph and looted wines.

"They have men on watch over the road. They can't have seen us. As soon as we can, we must move away."

Celestine pressed his shoulder, and as he leaned towards her whispered in a hardly audible voice, "There is someone to the left, behind us and further from the fire."

Beast, man and woman strained their ears, completely still. Then Porrott silently drew the loaded pistol from his belt. He heard a quick indrawn breath, and felt Celestine slip from her seat. Turning, he could not see her in the shadow, but sensed that a new figure had come out from the bushes. As he raised the pistol the moon broke through the branches and he saw it clearly – a small girl, crying, wet and muddy, plunging unsteadily towards the light and warmth.

Celestine darted into the exposed clearing; he saw she was on her knees beside the child, and swung his aim towards the unseen watchers over the road. They had not moved. The gun barrels were held, steady, blue in the moonbeams. They must see her. Then she picked up the little girl and glided back into the darkness. Sometime later she was at his side, holding up the child to him. Another movement in the shadows, and a second woman appeared. The child reached out to her and the woman took hold of it.

"Sir," she breathed, "Whoever you are, have pity on us. My man is hurt bad. He must find a surgeon or he will bleed to death. This way sir, I beg you." She set off before with the child.

He saw Celestine nod, and tug at the bridle. "I will walk with her. Do you follow close and keep us covered." She was gone in the woman's tracks, leaving him no choice.

After a while he saw them again, leaning over a man who was lying on the ground. They were now well beyond the light of the fire, but his eyes had grown accustomed to the darkness, so that even with a partly clouded moon it was possible to see what was before him. Porrott examined the man. It was clear he had been cruelly handled. His left arm lay at an awkward angle, his chest was crushed, blood trickled from his mouth and ran from a gash on his head into his eyes. As the woman wiped his face with a damp kerchief he recognised the man who had collected their toll the day before.

"You are from the cottage, mistress? Thank God you are all alive."

"Aye, but for how long? Can we take him to the surgeon? When they came bursting into our house they dragged us from our beds and- " her voice began to rise.

The sick man muttered and tossed about on the uneven ground. The child might wail at any moment. What were he and Celestine doing here, lingering in such peril? They could be safely away in a moment if he could only catch her up behind him. But she was kneeling by the man, trying to give him a drink, as steadily as if he was lying safely in bed. So he bit back his impatient words and deftly helped the sick man onto the horse, and slowly set off leading it. The man's wife walked by his side to support him, and Celestine carried the child – Nell it was called.

The woman knew her way. Soon they had left the moorland and were progressing along a steep-sided lane between fields. Perhaps there was no longer need for silence. It was to be hoped so, for there was no silence. He listened to the monotonous sound of the muffled hooves, forming themselves into silly patterns, and the horse's breathing, willing them to drown the man's intermittent moaning. If only he would be quiet. And then he was, and Porrott wondered if he was dead, and his wish for quiet had killed him. Down and along the winding lane. Not a situation for an ambitious young groom; not a rider for his master's horse. And he was so tired. Could he put the gun away now? Then he became aware of a gentle trickle of words behind him and realised that Celestine was telling Nell a story. He heard only occasional words but was steadied by the quiet, reassuring tone, which was lulling the three-year-old to sleep. He turned towards Celestine, her face just distinguishable, and knew that she smiled at him "Not so far now."

The woman stumbled. He looked at her and realised she was very near her time. "Mistress, would you care to lead the horse while I support your poor husband?" She changed places and the horse submitted to her leading. "We need to find both surgeon and constable. Do you know where they live?"

"Yes we must take him first to the surgeon, and then as you please. Indeed we must tell the constable. They dragged us from the house, and as you see my husband has been shamefully entreated. I thought they would have killed us all, but one man – aye, and one of the leaders too – he called them off. "We are not here to slaughter babes and women," he said, " and I for one would not slit a man's throat, however he might deserve it, in front of his wife and bairn, and let them see what fruit is on the tree!" They pulled us out of the house, and held us facing the fire, then they ransacked the house, dressed a bolster in my man's clothing and hanged it, yelling and jeering. Then in the confusion we slipped away into the wood, and my husband fell and could not move from where you found us. They were all of them like devils in their madness. – but I have seen more than one scar, and the constable may-"

"Now mistress, think well before you speak. This mob

has destroyed your home but spared your lives. If you send any to the gallows for this, will the next turnpike mob leave any to tell the tale? Believe me, it will be best to say – truly that you were terrified and confused and – perhaps less truly - that you recall nothing clearly. It is dangerous to say too much, or to say what you suspect."

She was silent for a while, then: "At least I will say nothing until John is well enough to give me his advice."

The sky was showing lighter grey bars near the horizon by the time they were outside the surgeon's house. Celestine said firmly, "I will go in with them. Do you rouse the constable and bring him here. They must not travel further tonight."

He watched her enter the house with them, then rode for the constable. He was not easy to waken, nor quick of understanding when awake, and it was almost an hour before Porrott could bring him to the surgeon's house by which time the wounded man was dressed and drugged, and his family safely asleep.

The surgeon refused to rouse them, but gave a brief account of the man's injuries. Porrott described the scene at the turnpike – the fire, the hooded figures, the effigy – but perhaps forgetting in his fatigue, perhaps abiding by the warning he had given the woman, made no mention of the armed watchers. The constable was indignant that this further outrage should follow so closely upon the druid's death, but was hopeful that the two events were connected.

"I expect the leaders of this mob killed the old man also. Yet this in no way agrees with the rumours I had heard."

"Rumours, sir?"

"Aye they say there was a woman seen in the grounds of the hall that night."

Porrott laughed shortly. "Have a care, do you mean the headless nun, the sorrowful queen, or the weeping girl? They have all been seen and sworn to by late carousing yokels. I doubt the fellow was killed by a ghost."

"And so do I. But for all that, what good would a woman be about in the grounds at night? She must be found and questioned."

"But have you thought that a conscientious gamekeeper might find a ghost or two most serviceable for safeguarding his master's pheasants. Only the other day I heard his Lordship avow that he was heartily sick of ghostly tales about the grounds, and if he heard of anyone else spreading tales of mysterious women in the vicinity he would horsewhip the man himself, be he pauper or magistrate. So have a care where you repeat that story!"

"Nay, I daresay it was but idle talk. I shall call upon your patients later, to hear their tales, and will send men to the site of the turnpike gates. I may need you two again but you can both go now."

They arrived home unseen as the cocks were crowing, too tired for speech or thought.

A few hours later Lord Fenborough's coach set out along the same road. This conveyance was even more crowded than on the day before, for sending one horse back with Porrott (who had ridden on the box with the coachman) necessitated his Lordship travelling with the ladies.

Moreover, there were many extra parcels and packets, particularly noticeable being a wicker basket with bars at the front held somewhat gingerly on Leonie's lap.

Lord Fenborough regarded the basket with much distaste. He had not been pleased when his wife noticed the young sailor with the marmoset and insisted on buying the creature. "Look my dear! A marmoset just like Christina's. I was mightily taken with the beast and resolved to purchase one myself if the opportunity ever arose. Just look at its hands and little face! Christina tells me they are the most loveable little creatures, and all the rage at Bath."

His Lordship did recall his sister-in-law's raptures over the beast. He also recalled his brother-in-law's comments at the billiard table. But it was a pleasure to see his wife eager for once, and he had complied with a good grace. Now she was biting slices of crystallised fruit into small pieces and feeding it with them. A shockingly human, hairy little hand poked out from between the bars and snatched the morsels from her beringed white fingers. He averted his gaze, for it did not seem right that the two hands should touch. Both the girls were leaning forward, eagerly watching the little monkey. Leonie manifested her usual bland expression.

His Lordship was of the opinion, not uncommon among farmers, that animals had no place in the house, and should always repay the feeding in usefulness or cash. "Where will you keep it my dear? It can hardly be given the run of the drawing room?"

"But do you not recall? Christina had the most elegant little stand fashioned, and her pet was attached to it by a fine chain round its waist. It climbed down to the floor and up again but it could not run wild. I have been thinking, we shall commission Mr Chippendale to make us one in gilded wood. I would like it to be shaped like a palm tree arising from an island, with Neptune and his sea-nymphs around the base blowing conches. And we have it by the window so that dear Jacko can see out – won't we my precious?"

Lord Fenborough wondered what incident would terminate this arrangement. A vase left within reach, a tugged handful of my lady's hair, a Chinese rug ruined? Then it would fall to him to decide what to do with the beast. She would not have her discarded pet destroyed.

"Ah he is cunning" Araminta cried. "Are you thinking of keeping him in the aviary ma'am? It would be warm and pleasant for him, and he could talk with the little parakeets.

While his wife insisted that her little Jacko would stay with her always he considered Araminta's suggestion. It seemed a reasonable solution – but who was to look after it once his wife had grown tired of cutting up fruit on a porcelain plate? Certainly not any of his grooms; they had real work to do and so had his gamekeepers. Then he thought of the matching pair of little black pages his wife had acquired last year to stand beside her with her tray of chocolate. They had plenty of time, it was suitable work for children, and if they turned out to be good with animals he could, when they had grown too tall and awkward for the drawing room, put them to work himself.. It would be a kindness to the lads for all boys should have the care of beasts, and he might gain himself two distinguished looking, well trained grooms. Letty's friend was a pleasant little thing and not such a goose as she looked. He leaned forward to speak to her.

"And have you enjoyed your outing, Araminta?"

"Oh sir, I have. I do thank you for your kindness. Do you know, I have never really been to the theatre before?"

"No indeed, Minta, you forget. We were all taken by Mrs Martindale in York once. I forget the play but I remember the lace trimming I put on my bonnet for the occasion."

"But that was at school! We all had to walk in twos, with the teachers before and behind, like Noah and Mrs Noah and all the animals!. This is the first real visit, Besides, we had to go whether we would or not. And it was a foolish, trifling piece I recall, with little but splendid clothes to interest the audience, and a silly girl ready to die for love, when there was no need for it at all. But this was much better. I shall never forget the witches, and the scene where the woman takes the daggers from her poor weak husband, to put them by the king's body. I am sure I could never do such a thing – even for a husband I loved as she loved him. But if I did, I hope I would not run mad and see ghosts and betray everything."

"I should hope not, Minta. 'Tis no way for a lady to conduct herself. But perhaps when the play was first writ ladies were less refined. I cannot imagine any woman of breeding being so fierce and formidable or so coarse in her speech. What do you think, Mama?"

Lady Fenborough broke off a piece of banana, gave it to

Jacko, and wiped her fingers on a lace handkerchief before she replied. "I can hardly recall the story. I saw the play as a young woman and have no wish to see it again. I remember it as barbarous stuff, full of folly and violence. But I think a woman may be very taken aback by what she had brought herself to do. I think she might well run mad if…"

She stopped with a sharp exclamation and looked at Jacko. He had taken advantage of her momentary abstraction to delve into the bag she carried at her waist and remove a shining trinket. This he licked and tried with his teeth.

Alarmed, she tried to coax it back from him. He jerked it away, and as she moved to grasp his paw he made as if to swallow it. At once all four women were leaning forward, trying to persuade him to put down what he had taken.

Araminta took out of her bag a shining pencil and held it out in her right hand. She waved it enticingly before him, and the little coloured tassel at the end swung round. He watched it. She held it almost out of reach, so that he would have to hold on to the bars with one hand and stretch out with the other if he was to take it. Gradually his right hand came out still clenched. Then, swiftly he had dropped his prize and grabbed the pencil. An emerald and diamond earring lay in Araminta's lap for a moment, then her Ladyship whisked it away and dropped it back into her bag with trembling fingers. "I feared the diamond had come loose and took it to a jeweller's for repair. I hope the little brute has not harmed it … poor Jacko, he didn't know any better, did he?"

There was silence for a while as the coach lurched along.

Leonie was gloomily working out how to keep her mistress's jewels and cosmetics safe from her new pet. Araminta was wondering how to ask Lord Fenborough if he thought it was ever possible for people to see into the future like the witches in the play – not by magic of course, but perhaps by some kind of science like magnetism , or some electrical power, when the coach came to a standstill.

All looked out upon the devastation of the burnt out cottage. Shattered scorched pages and broken household stuff littered the roadside. As Araminta looked in the window where the day before she had seen Nell and her doll she saw only smouldering rubbish. A number of the constable's men were searching through the ruins. Lord Fenborough, a magistrate, stepped down and was soon in consultation with the man in charge of proceedings. While the remaining human occupants of the coach leaned out to see what they could, Jacko took advantage of their distraction to withdraw the wooden pegs from the front of his prison, push open the lid and leap out through the window. He vanished into the trees, reappeared running along a branch, swung on the tattered effigy that still dangled from the tree and was gone again. The lady's shriek brought her husband to her side. With controlled exasperation he set the constable's men to capture the escaped prisoner and soon, chattering furiously, Jacko was safely returned to his basket. After sitting with his back to the company for a while he reached out and tugged Araminta's dress. As she looked at him he held out a closed paw and put into her hand a gold tiepin set with rubies.

"Oh look! He has brought me a present in exchange for

the pencil. But whatever should I do with it?"

"I think I had best hand it back to the searchers if it was found here, "Lord Fenborough remarked. "Strange," examining it closely, "I would not expect to find this in a turnpike cottage. It looks to me as if it could be part of a footpad's horde."

A few minutes later he was back again. "Oh sir, when did it happen ?"

"Late last night. But you need not be concerned for your maid. It seems she and Porrott came by after the deed but managed to escape notice. Indeed it was they who brought the turnpike family safely to the village."

"Oh Papa, Papa, has anyone been killed?"

"No, it seems they did no murder. But for all that, once we catch the miscreants they will hang as high as that poor bolster there. It was by the Hand of Providence alone that the people in the cottage escaped. Do you all continue home. I will stay here for a while to see that all is done as it should be."

Araminta hoped the little girl had saved her doll.

Wednesday night

My dearest Louisa,

This has been a day of great turmoil and excitement and, now that it is over, I will own to you alone, of some peril. I was so afeard for a while, but all is now happily resolved. As I write by the fire Celestine is stitching away with might and main and my gown is well on the way. She hopes to have time to make a lace edging for the sleeves.

My lady has purchased the strangest creature , a furry little monkey with a long tail and a parti-coloured face, called a marmoset. He is very pretty, but will lead us a merry dance with his thieving ways. He caused great excitement in the coach with his snatching of pretty trinkets. I hope he does not miss the young sailor boy she bought him from, for he sat cosily within his coat peering out and chattered most distressingly when he was taken out and set in the far colder arms of Leonie. She dislikes him, but since it is she who must tend him and he is likely to prove a difficult charge it is easy to understand her aversion.

The journey home bade fair to be most enjoyable at first but alas! As we came up to the turnpike cottage we beheld – imagine our horror, dear sister – that it had been burnt to the ground. The family with the little girl were forced to flee into the night! Lord Fenborough seems confident that the miscreants will soon be caught. I do not think I shall feel really safe until they are. Celestine, who had been sent on ahead, tells me they came upon the scene of riotous destruction and by the guidance , no doubt, of a merciful

Providence, both escaped and were able to lead the poor family to safety. The man was sorely hurt, but my pity is for the woman who was very near her time, and the poor babe of about three years, who understood nothing of the night's work but that she must keep quiet. Celestine tells me there have been other riots in the countryside. Only a year ago a harmless enough man – one of the wandering Methodist preachers- was set upon by a mob as he was peacefully riding to preach, and was dragged from his horse, thrown in the river and left for dead, with such injuries and broken bones that he barely made his escape, poor fellow,

I own to you that I would fain have spent today quietly at home, for the day was cold and windy at first and we had had excitement and travel enow over the last two days, but hardly had Celestine finished pinning me into the new gown before the fire in my room – and it is going to be really beautiful – I do wish there was an ardent young portrait painter who would see me in it and be moved to request the honour of painting me in all my finery – when Letty came in, all excitement, to tell me that Frederick and his friend William would like us to be ready in half an hour to ride with them. So I changed into my habit and wrapped up warm. You will realise how cold it was when I tell you I prepared myself to ride with these two young men with far more concern for warmth than appearance – and it was as well I did.

Once we had set out I began to take pleasure in our ride. For a while the sun appeared amid the clouds, giving us little warmth but cheerful light, and when I saw the bourne whither we were bound I was indeed glad we had come.

It is a place called Brim Ham Rocks, over towards Pateley Bridge but high up on the moors.

Picture yourself, dear Louisa, picking your way through tufts of dying heather and seeing suddenly ahead of you, rising as it were like rugged cliffs out of the heathy billows a great number of rude and rugged piles of stones, many times the height of a man, with fissures, and clefts and holes you can see the sky through. All the edges of the rocks have been twisted into grotesque shapes by the winds of the centuries, and each massy pile seemed more awe-inspiring than the last, as we quietly wended our way between them.

At last we came to a little valley, surrounded by six or seven of these stone giants, and dismounted awhile. From where we sat, one of the rocks looked from the side like a grim, stony face, so amazing that I wished to make a sketch of it. I thought perhaps I might later make it into a memento of my visit and bring it home for Mama. Letty had not her pencils with her but was willing to sit at the bottom of the rock. I was pleased with the contrast between her pretty, gentle face and the harsh rock behind. The horses were left to the groom and the young men set off to scramble among the rocks. (How shocked they would all have been had I yielded to temptation, kicked off my shoes, kilted up my skirts and followed them as I did when we all went to Conistone five years ago. But alas these young men are not brothers and cousins, and I am now a woman grown.)

I had not been long at my sketch when I looked up to see that the top of the rock had disappeared, and the figure of Letty was partly dissolving in a sudden thick mist. I called out, and she ran back to join me. By the time I had packed my satchel we could see no more than a few feet before us. The wind had entirely dropped; there was no sound to be heard except the distant , chill piping of a solitary bird. The swirling mists really made the rocks look as if they were leaning towards us, ready to fall on our heads. We were on our own in the midst of a little circle of heath, with billowing mists blinding us to all beyond, safe when momentarily we caught a glimpse of a towering, rocky mass, now at the front, now at the side, now – it seemed – creeping up on us from behind. We clasped each other for warmth, and listened for our companions. No sound of man or horse, yet they could not be far away. Letty called out to her brother. The fog swallowed up the thin sound. We both called again and again, the silence between our cries eddying back to us in the white, drizzling mist. Then I thought I heard the jingle of a harness, but was not sure, nor of the direction, yet made to move towards where it might be. Letty begged me not to move for fear of falling over a precipice.

Then we heard a distant ululation, a rising and falling to chill the blood. In that uncanny place we were both like little children, terrified of the strange creatures of nursery tales. "Surely that cannot be –"I had begun when Letty shrieked aloud. A second later I too heard breathings behind us and felt a tap on the shoulder. We tried to run but were held by strong arms.

Terrifying as this was, there was some comfort. For the arms were solid. I had feared their touch would pass through us (Yes you may smile, sitting as you are at home by the fire) Then we heard laughter, human laughter, and William's voice.

"For shame Frederick! 'Tis a pity to scare them so. I am sorry for my part ladies, you were so taken aback. 'Twas but a foolish jest."

"Scared, sir?" I made shift to reply. "Perhaps a little startled for you came up so quietly, but we are not babies to be frightened by a little fog, are we Laetitia?"

Letty was clinging to her brother and weeping. He, I thought, seemed a little ashamed. "Come now, Letty, no harm's done. Compose yourself you little goose, we must be finding our way home. Can you see the confounded horse, William? What the devil is Walker doing?"

William replied he had last seen the groom leading the horses down the valley for a drink. He would probably be waiting caught in the fog himself or perhaps keeping deliberately below the mist.

We set off down the valley. It was thoroughly unpleasant walking for the heathery tufts were full of water drops which soaked our feet and draggled our skirts horribly. Darkness would soon be falling. The four of us walked closely together, the men calling out to the groom at intervals. I do not know how long we were struggling along. Twice we were in water above the ankle. The misty rain had soaked through all my garments and I was altogether as uncomfortable and miserable as I have ever been.

Then we rounded a corner, and saw a few yards in front of us a small fire with people around it and a larger looming shape behind. It was too late to turn aside, for men rose up with lanterns and came towards us. They brought us to the fire, and I saw to my alarm, that we had fallen in with a band of wandering gypsies. Wild and rough they looked indeed – very like I had always imagined and though I had often longed to encounter such people I wished then far enough away now. So many adventures are delightful on the page but terrifying in the flesh. The leader spoke to Frederick, and it was clear that he recognised Lord Fenborough's son. They were very civil to us and made room for us by the fire. One of the lads was sent to find the horses. I noticed how sure footedly he moved in the mist. By now Letty and I were shaking with the cold, and an old woman invited us into the van.

"Best go in," murmured William, "But keep hold of your purses. Whatever their intentions for good or ill, his Lordship's name will be your safeguard. They must understand they will be justly rewarded for any good or ill they do to us."

We followed the old woman into the van and accepted the blankets she wrapped round us. As we sat (on the floor) she brought us some broth which she had been cooking on the fire. I daresay the dish was none too clean and the flavour was unfamiliar, but we were too cold and hungry to be nice, and took it with gratitude. When we saw her close, I do not suppose she was so very old, for her daughter of about fourteen was in the van. She was making lace by candlelight. She looked up quickly and smiled at us. I thought she would have been pretty if she had been cleaner and better dressed. It was warm in the van and I felt myself drowsy. I could hear William and Frederick outside, talking about horseracing with the gypsies.

I must have closed my eyes for a moment, for the next time I looked up I saw the old woman had hold of one of Letty's hands. She was holding it, palm upward, near the light of another candle, and in her eyes was such a look – as if she was staring right through the veins and creases. The pink hand lay in the brown one; I noticed the black and torn nails. The dark hand was still as a rock, the pink trembled a little. Very quietly the woman spoke.

This is not a fortunate hand, my lady. Are you sure you wish to know what it tells me?" I saw Letty's bent head nod. A deep sigh, and the dirty hand became rigid, clasping the other. I saw Letty try to pull her hand away, but she could not. Red marks appeared on her hand where the other's fingers dug in. "Within seven days" – the grasp became inexorable, the woman leaned towards Letty and seemed to compel her to raise her head. Black eyes pierced blue, and Letty could not turn away - "seven days, you will lose for ever that for which you live." Then, suddenly, she let go the hand and turned away. Letty was released to hide her face.

And I? Should I call out to them? Did I want to know what was in store for me? Then it came to me that I was dreaming, and recalling the play I had seen. And I know also from that play that no good ever comes of looking into the future, though there are things I would fain know, so I held my peace.

The next thing I knew was a hallooing from outside at the return of the horses and we rode home in a great bustle. The fog was lifted. I tried to look closely at my friend but it was too dark to see her face clearly. She spoke not a word, and I wondered if she had had the same dream. For it must have been a dream, must it not, Louisa? I do not really think that anyone can foretell the future, but before you laugh too loud at me, remember the moor, and the rocks, and the cold mist.

My very best love to you all,
Araminta

* * *

That evening Celestine wrote about the day just past.
Wednesday night

I have often smiled to myself as I watched my young
mistress scribbling away, and wondered at her eagerness to
impart every detail of her day to her friends and relations,
but today I find myself envying her. I too am bewildered
and uncertain what to do for the best – afraid for her and
for my own life – and there is no-one to whom I can turn
for advice or pour out my troubles. So I thought I would
imitate the young ladies in another way and keep me a
journal. I am grateful that my mother taught me to write
a good hand, and that God gave me the power to set out
my thoughts in words. I am using the back pages of the
notebook I have to keep account of our expenditure. I am
writing for myself alone, none but my eyes shall read this...

Where shall I start? If only I could talk to my sensible
mistress and ask her counsel. I wish I could know if I am
right in suspecting that someone knows where we were
and what we saw on Friday night. Perhaps I should make
a clean breast of it all to the constable, but Porrott tells
me that would be a foolish courting of danger. When I
was a little girl I once went a walk with my mother, up
onto the fell to collect some fine woollen cloth an old lady
produced for us to sell in the shop. The sun was shining and
white clouds raced across a bright blue sky, and the wind
whipped the skirt of my new red coat around my ankles.
Maman was walking briskly along the track, leading the
packhorse and singing one of the songs I had heard from
the cradle "Il était une bergère" while I skipped along from

stone to stone up the course of a winding stream. I recall how happy I felt, how comfortable the cloak in the wind and sun. Then I jumped, both feet together, on to a big green tussock on the bank - landed in mud to my knees, and fell headlong, twisting my ankle badly. The shock, the cold, the pain and the dirty brown splashes on my new cloak filled me with grief and terror and it was a long time before I durst leap about in the sun again. I feel the same now. How can I have confidence in any familiar action, or take any person at face value, having been plunged into the cold miriness of this violent death? I reassure Araminta, and watch her relax and forget her fears for half an hour, but who shall reassure me?

And should I not rather urge her to be on guard at all times? If only I were her older sister I would have authority to take her home forthwith, but alas I am not and must do my best to shield her from her uncertainties and caprices. I pray God we both come home safe, but I fear she will never again be as thoughtlessly happy as she was when we came here.

This afternoon I watched from the window of our room the arrival of the constable's man in the courtyard. He was tall and broad with a red pimpled face and thick lips. He held the reins clumsily with stubby fingers, and dismounted with a thump. That thump echoed in my heart. I was sure he had come to find out more about the mysterious woman in the grounds at night. I saw Porrott lead away his horse, and then one of the indoor servants came to conduct him to the estate office.

A few minutes later came a tap at the door. It was Sarah, a girl of about fourteen. She was scared and excited.

"Please, miss, the constable's man here and wants to talk to you in the estate office."

Porrott was waiting for me in the courtyard. "Try not to look so afraid," he murmured. "The man is a complete fool, Most of the constable's men are busy out at the burnt-out cottage, and after ten minutes' talk I can well see why he should be spared for a routine task such as getting our stories about last night. Courage, my girl. Remember, you are not a lady – no vapours or fainting fits!"

The officer made us both stand before him. I wondered if he could not hear my heartbeats or feel them vibrating through the stone floor. He took a long time preparing his quill. I could see he was not much at home with such an implement and my courage restored a little, so I was able to answer his questions about the previous night with fair composure. He made a little merry about why Porrott and I should be alone together at such an hour, but Porrott's steely "We were attending to his Lordship's express orders" soon cooled his mockery. I asked him about the woman and heard that she had just been delivered of a boy, which was not like to live. Then he coughed and arranged the tawdry lace of his cravat importantly. His thick red throat bulged over it.

"Now then my girl, tell me what you know about this old man that was killed here."

I told him, "My mistress and I had only arrived here on a visit a few days before his body was found, sir, and neither of us ever spoke with him."

"Ha! So no sooner had you got here than he was killed. You admit it! And which of you was it then that was lurking around -"

Porrott had been peering out of the window and his exclamation startled both of us. My interrogator turned his attention to him.

"What!, How dare you interrupt my business, business of the first importance?"

"I do beg your pardon, sir, but it's them varmints of poachers. His Lordship told me special to look out for them and just now I seen a stealthy figure a-lurking in the woods, and I thought as how you, being as it were the law in these parts –"

The constable's neck swelled like a turkey cock and a gratified beam appeared over his face, to be replaced by a solemn judicious look, as befitted an embodiment of the law. In response to Porrot's rough speech his the more aped gentility; "Where, where, my good man? Good heavens, you dolt, don't waste my time with hesitation. You must conduct me immediately to the exact location. I will happrehend the felon forthwith and at once. You had better go back to your work, girl. Beyond doubt 'tis no mere poacher but the same hidentical hassassin we have just glimpsed."

He abandoned pen and notes in his haste. Porrott picked them up and handed them back with a bow, helped him on with the cloak he had thrown onto a chair and ushered him out of the door. As he set off to follow him towards the densest part of the thicket the look fixed on his shoulder blades was certainly at odds with his deferential tones.

I lost no time in returning to my work. I had done as much as I could to the gown without a fitting, so I took out my bobbins and began a lace edging of poppies and sheaves of corn for the neck and sleeves. I sat in the window and was not at all surprised to see the two men returning about an hour later, empty-handed – if you discount the visitor's right hand which clasped lovingly an empty pocket-flask. Porrott helped him onto his horse with some difficulty, and he was borne away lurching from side to side as if his horse were a small boat in a choppy sea. I think it is likely that in a few hours' time he would feel as if he had indeed been in such a vessel, unless he fall off and brake his neck in the interval.

When he had gone I opened the window, Porrott looked up, and I asked him to tell me what had befallen. He came into my room grinning.

"That's seen that fat fool off. By the time we had chased shadows all through the wood, and I had replenished his flask from mine (Frederick for all his faults keeps good brandy and does not keep as close a check on it as I would in his position) he knew not what day it was, nor whether he was searching for man, woman or orang-utan. I told him he was a fine officer and I would commend his zeal to his Lordship. When he comes to himself he will long to forget the morning's work. He will want nothing from us except to be left alone. I think we can oblige him in that readily enough.

"So, as I thought, there wasn't anyone lurking in the woods, was there?"

"Not so far as I know, not then. But there had been ."

"What do you mean?"

Porrott pulled a few strands of wool from his pocket. "What do you think of this?"

I told him I thought it might be wool from a stray sheep.

"It might be, except that I found it caught on a twig nearly six feet from the ground above the faint track that leads from the Druid's cave to the Temple of Piety. And in some places lichen had been rubbed off the trees, and in others there were signs as if some heavy object had been dragged along – possibly in a sack."

So it seemed likely that someone had moved the body, or at least had been behaving strangely in the wood. Probably someone who had a greyish wig .... Or could get their hands on one… which meant in fact almost anybody.

"Porrott", I said, "that rubbed lichen. It must have caught on someone's clothes. Surely one of the servants may have noticed, may have had to clean off stains."

"Unfortunately," he replied coolly, "there has been no trace of mud or lichen on any of Frederick's clothing or boots. You may rest assured I would have seen it as it is the young man's whim to have the same servant for groom and valet. A pity but there it is. We can, I suppose keep our ears and eyes open but the state of one's employer's clothing is not a common topic of conversation among servants."

I must have looked shocked, and carried on with my

work in silence. He wandered over to the fire and kicked the logs further back into the grate "Well, I have never pretended I have any opinion of my master. He is a wild and evil young man. It would be no shock to me to find him involved in any villainy, but facts are facts. I know what clothing he had with him and it is all accounted for."

I reminded him hesitatingly that he had been away the previous day. He nodded, and said cheerfully that it might have been possible for him to have had his clothing attended to by somebody else in that time.

"And indeed this might help us find out the truth ! If I make enquiries among the female servants and you among the male….my poor little Minta is driven half frantic with terror. If only we can find out what really happened."

He laughed shortly. "You seem mighty devoted to that little minx. More like an elder sister than a maid.. What's that you are doing for her now?" He came towards me and watched the lace forming around the bobbins for a while. "That's skillful , that is. I never saw anyone making lace before. Who taught you how to do it?"

"My mother."

"And there's another thing, Celestine. When I took you to the constable's man I rallied you, saying you could not faint because you were not a lady and yet you seem to me to be more like a lady in the way you act and talk than I think one in your station should be."

I could perhaps have turned this as a little compliment with a laugh, but I delayed for too long, staring in to the fire. Then I found myself telling this near stranger what

I have never spoken of to anyone else, and he listened patiently while I unpacked the life that had been hidden away for twelve years.

I told him how my mother was the daughter of a wealthy cloth-merchant in the Low Countries who had fallen in love with a young Englishman sent to our Bruges warehouse to buy supplies for his master. In the end their determination broke down her parents' objections. They had intended her to marry the son of a leading banker and had educated her to that end, but they gave way at her threats to starve herself or enter a convent if she could not wed my father. Finally they allowed the marriage and settled on her an amount sufficient to allow her and my father to open their own mercer's shop in Kendal. So she came to England with her husband and set to work to learn a new language and a whole new way of life. She told me later she was perfectly happy for seven years, until a farm cart ran away in the main street and crushed my father against a wall. I was five years old at the time. She carried on the shop alone, for she was a most capable woman and educated me by teaching me what she had been taught. We read many English books together, for although we sometimes spoke French at home she was determined I should speak like an Englishwoman. From the time I was eight or nine I used to help in the shop. Once or twice a year Araminta's mother would come into our shop to buy silks and laces, and she liked me to serve her – my mother always at hand to help, of course.

"And she took a fancy to you and took you into her household? Why ever did your mother let you go?"

I went on to tell him of my mother's fatal illness, leaving me an orphan at the age of twelve. "My mother's brother heard of her sickness and arrived with his wife and two daughters on the day she died. I am glad now she did not know of their arrival. He had never forgiven my mother. They took over the business at once. My aunt was not kind to me. I think it was because her own girls, though older than I, were of much less use in the shop. Perhaps too she was jealous of one who had married for love and had some years of happiness. My aunt and uncle disagreed about me; she wanted me out of sight in the kitchen while he wanted me useful behind the counter, because I was quick with figures and knew how to be pleasing to the customers. One day when I was serving Mrs Lewthwaite came in. She asked me to measure out ten yards of a fine blue figured velvet, and asked me if anything ailed my mother, as she was not in the shop. At her kind words, the first I had heard for months, the tears spilled out down my face and bounced onto the cloth I was measuring. I can still see the wet splashes. I turned my head away but my uncle saw what had happened and the ruined velvet. He snatched up his clothyard and struck me on the head with it several times. I heard him trying to apologise in his clumsy English: 'I am so regretting, dear madam. It is a wicked girl to ruin your so lovely cloth. She cry for her mother death, the foolish girl.'

"By now I was crouched beneath the counter, my head in my hands, determined that he should not hear me weeping. I heard my mistress, in a voice I did not recognise and have never since heard, say, 'Sir, one who accounts it folly for a child to weep at her mother's death is a beast and no man, and of all creatures the least fitted to have care of a child.' Then they talked together quietly. After a while he summoned my aunt and all three spoke together for some time.

"The upshot was that Mrs Lewthwaite took me aside and asked me if I would go with her to be trained as her maid. To exchange meagre food, carping criticism , scorn and blame for a safe home where I would not hear my mother reviled constantly. Of course I went with her gladly. She has been as good as her word. For twelve years she has provided for me and I have been happy to serve first her and now her daughter, whom, as you have noticed, I love like a sister."

"But why did they take no steps to recover your inheritance for you?"

"Within a year my uncle and aunt had bankrupted the shop, and when my mother married it seems she gave up all right to bequeath any property in exchange for her settlement. My lady told me of this when I was of an age to understand. She told me at the same time that she hoped I would remain with her for good, or until I wished to marry a suitable young man."

"If she is so indulgent to you, it seems to me that you are slow to consult your own interests – has Araminta no older brothers for you to captivate?"

"For shame, sir! Do you think me such a base ingrate? I own that her two brothers might, with a little encouragement …but pleasant young men as they are, I have known them too long and like them too well to wish to make use of either of them in that way. Besides, it would greatly hurt my lady. And moreover, I am taller than one, and the other has ginger whiskers!"

Porrott looked thoughtful. "I can see why you so honour your mistress now. I find it a strange story, and far from my experience. Then after a long pause, "I was not so fortunate as you as a child."

I could do nothing but ask him if he wished to talk about his own childhood. He sat poking the fire, never looking at me. He was quiet for so long I thought he had decided to hold his peace .but at last he began.

"I never knew my mother. An aunt brought me up. I never knew my father either. When I was little I believed he had died also, for my aunt and uncle, who had six other children to bring up and little enough money to do it on found time to tell me little beyond my mother's name. But when I was ten another aunt came on a visit and she told me – nobody knew who my father was. In a childish way this rather pleased me. Whenever I saw a gentleman ride by I thought to myself 'You could be my father' and when the young gentlemen of my own age from the nearby academy swaggered by with their fine coats I would watch them closely and wonder which of them might be my brother. I took pains to perfect my reading and writing as best I could, in case my father should ever be in a position to acknowledge me, for I did not wish him to be ashamed of his son. Perhaps it was partly to search for him that I sought work as a manservant, and for some years took service with various young men of birth and breeding. By now I had become convinced that I had noble blood, and was confident that in person, intelligence and manners I was inferior to none, despite my livery coats."

He sank into silence again, so as to prompt him I asked, "And what happened then? I can see that something happened to trouble and disturb you."

"My grandmother died. My employer at that time was visiting a country house not five miles from where I had been brought up and one of my old neighbours saw me and told me about her death. I took myself to the funeral, for I remembered her being as kind to me as she could, beset as she was by poverty and numerous grandchildren. Afterwards I met again the aunt who had given me what information I had about my birth. In our talk I perhaps spoke too warmly of my unknown father, and my wish to know him one day. She told me I had no business to feel so kindly towards him. 'I may not know his name, but I can tell you what sort of man he was.' Celestine, she told me - with gloating – that my poor mother had been barely twelve when I was born. One day she had set out to do an errand in the village and when she did not return her father set out to look for her, and found her dishevelled, bleeding and half out of her mind weeping and shrieking by the roadside. She could never bring herself to talk about the man who attacked her...... they took her to an old woman who gave her a draught to procure an abortion, but it did not work and seven months later I was born – the child of rape, and she died. The man I had been so eager to find! The man I had striven to be worthy of! I hope to God I never do meet him, for if I do, I will kill him. That poor girl!"

I could find no words and he shook off my hand.

"So now I knew, more or less, who I was, and I saw no further good in improving myself. I did not go back to my master, but made my way to London, bitterly sorry I had ever been born. I was afraid I might be like him. For that fear I never since looked at a woman. After a time I had to work. Always before I had looked for an employer from whom I could learn something useful, but now I took what Fate sent me. And after I had worked for a foolish young fop, Fate sent me Frederick. A depraved master for a tainted man."

He frightened me; I have never seen into a man's soul and heart before, and know not what to say or do. I cannot recall what more was said, until the sounds of the coach's arrival broke in and, begging me to forget what he had told me, he rushed down to the courtyard with his face averted. Poor young man! When we meet it shall be on my part as if he had not told me.

The same evening Betty was sitting before the fire in her home with Nell on her knee. Earlier in the day a neighbour had run into the house with news of the attack on the turnpike, for the turnpike keeper's wife was Mrs Grainger's youngest sister. Betty and her mother had set off immediately for the cottage where the family had been taken, John driving them in his wagon. There was work for them there, for the child had just been born, and soon they heard from both man and wife about the horrors of the night that had just passed. Later it had been decided that Mrs Grainger should remain with her sister for a time, and

Betty should take Nell back home with her. The little girl had not been willing to leave her mother but after a while she sobbed herself to sleep in Betty's arms on the jolting ride back.

That evening she was laid out on a makeshift bed in the main room of the cottage but was soon awake, crying out with a bad dream, and refused to be laid down again. So Betty cuddled her, wrapped her in a blanket and rocked her gently until she slept. Betty looked down at the child's pale face and was filled with a sense of rage and compassion such as she had never felt before. How dare anyone treat a child so! She wondered who the two strangers were that had helped the desperate family in the night. Aunt Mary thought they were servants at the Hall. She did not think who the man could be, but wondered if the young woman, who had her hair done in a way her aunt had never seen before and had an odd way of speaking might be the visiting young lady's maid that she had met in such strange circumstances on Friday night. If it was the same person she could have been involved in nothing bad, however strange her behaviour might appear. Aunt Mary had described how this stranger had stopped Nellie from wandering back into sight of the mob when she herself had not been able to reach her child and dared not call out to her. Then she had carried her for hours through the night to safety. No wicked girl would behave like that.

The door creaked and John came in, with Uncle Marmaduke and her father. She made as if to set the child down to lay out the supper.

"Nay lass, no need to disturb the poor bairn. Us men are not so helpless as all that." Her father set out the soup and bread on the table, said grace and they all ate hungrily, in silence.

Then the older men stretched out their legs before the fire and lit their pipes. Betty's grandmother lay between sleeping and waking, in the shadowed box-bed. John came to sit by Betty.

She turned to him eagerly. "Have you any news for me? Does anyone know who did this to our Mary and her family?"

John shook his head. "It's never easy to find out who has been doing this kind of thing, you know. People are ashamed in the cold light of day, and frightened womenfolk keep a good guard on their tongues lest the constable should discover their man was a-wandering in the night time. There has been some wild talk among the mining lads of what they would like to do to the new road and its tolls, but none now eager to claim he has fulfilled his drunken boasting. And if anyone knows a neighbour was abroad last night he is saying nothing. You remember how we never found out who threw our good friend Thomas Lee in the river when he came to preach, and that was in broad daylight. But there are many young men with their blood up, flown with excitement and wine. There was a group making a great noise in the tavern as I went by."

"Did you not see who any of them were?"

"I had no leisure to stay and join them. As far as I could see they were strangers to me, and although they were roaring and clapping each other on the back I heard nothing clearly to suggest they were in last night's mob. But I can tell you they all seemed mighty pleased with themselves."

Uncle Marmaduke joined in. "I heard there was now a mob getting together for another purpose." He knocked out his pipe on the hearth and took his time relighting it. "The gypsies are back on the moors again, and you know it is not their regular time to be here. Some are saying that they have come with a purpose."

"And why should the gypsies concern themselves with burning turnpikes? They follow other roads" John asked.

"And after all, " put in Mr Grainger, " 'tis not the way they behave. Poachers and thieves they may be, but I have never known them banded together in a howling and violent mob."

"Nay, you do not understand. Listen now, and I'll tell you." Uncle Marmaduke was enjoying their attention. "I came across old Mother Hardisty talking with her friends on the green, and she was crying out that the gypsies had ill-wished the old druid, and that had driven him to his death. She says she saw a young gypsy woman shake her fist and cry out upon him at the crossroads not a fortnight ago."

"Vain superstition," snorted Mr Grainger. "How do you suppose that brought about his death? Though by all accounts she may well have had cause to curse the man, as had so many others. Are they still believing in stories of charms and witches in these modern days?"

"There's witches in the Bible, " objected Uncle

Marmaduke, "why can they not be in Pateley as well? 'Tis ungodly to say there are none when they be there plain in Holy Writ."

"There's vines and figtrees in the Bible too, but I've never seen them in Pateley and I don't expect too." said John sharply. "And what did Anne Hardisty's gossips have to say to such foolishness."

"They were very impressed by what she had to say. One recalled she had turned away a gypsy woman selling pegs last week and next day three of her hens had died, and another that her sister's son had thrown a stone at the same woman and the day after had been in great pain in his belly. And just as they were all crying out together a good number of young men came by from the tavern. They listened to what the woman said and vowed to go out there and then to capture the witch and call her to account. Listen, can you not hear? The hunt is afoot and not far from here."

A whooping and hallooing were heard in the distance along the valley bottom. "'Twill go hard with the poor wench if they catch her, but I'm thinking they may be too fuddled to do aught but fall over their own feet. Maybe 'tis by the working of Providence that though overmuch ale gives a man foolish ideas it as often as not stops him from carrying them out."

As they listened the sounds died away. The room felt safe and peaceful again. Nell stirred and muttered in her sleep, and the fire began to burn low.

"John, lad, will you mend the fire? Bring in some logs from the pile beside the byre."

John went out with the lantern willingly enough, but within two minutes he was back, with no logs in his arms. He closed the door carefully and came uncertainly towards the fire. He licked his lips, and turned to his host.

"She's in our byre. I heard a rustling in the straw and thought as how the beasts were restless. And when I shone the lantern in I saw her crouched in a corner. She cannot be above twelve or thirteen years of age. And listen. I think the hunters are coming back. Pray God they have no dogs.

"'Thou shalt not suffer a witch to live' it says in the Book. Let us forget what John has seen and take no hand in it. Then if they take her 'twill be by the Will of God. 'Tis none of our business and we have no cause to meddle in such matters." Uncle Marmaduke spoke complacently but John turned to Mr Grainger.

"What shall we do, sir? Like I said this gypsy is but a child and she is terrified. I do not like to think how they will handle her if they have the chance, for men in drink are not men but beasts. But if they suspect we may be hiding her, what then? We have Betty and the children and an old woman under this roof."

Betty looked hard at her father. Had Nell been saved from one mob to fall to another? Mr Grainger took his time to reply, and while they waited the shouting grew nearer.

"I remember once the old parson telling me that in the old days any that got into a church was safe from justice whatever he had done, for that a church is a holy place where God has his dwelling. But then so too a byre is a holy place, and for the sake of Him who was born in a byre

I will not give up any that seeks sanctuary there. If they come up here I will be out in the yard. No John, not you, for I can say truly I have seen no stranger and you cannot. You stay here to protect those within the house.

The confused yelling came closer. Mr Grainger took a lantern out into the yard, and leaning on a pitchfork, went to the gate. He began to shift a pile of straw in the yard. The listeners in the warm room heard his tread and the sound of the straw moving, sounds soon drowned by the crashing and yells of the approaching crowd. They heard him greet the first arrivals.

"Why, Jem, you're out late tonight. Too drunk to find your way home?"

They could not make out the other words but heard the reply.

"Nay, Jem, I've not seen a soul, nor heard aught out of the ordinary but the racket you and your companions are making. You had best get home and cool your heads for it's a long day's work tomorrow. Come, talk a little sense, man, if you can. And you, Jack, Go on, back home with the lot of you. Look for your fairies and witches when it's light enough to see what you are about, you great fools. I warrant the thick heads you'll all have tomorrow will owe more to ale than to sorcery."

The leaders turned away; the rest followed. They could be heard stumbling down the bank. One man fell headlong and swore roundly. His friends laughed at him. Gradually the shouts died away and did not return.

Much later that night, after John and Uncle Marmaduke

had left, and all the others in the house were asleep. Betty cautiously opened the door of the byre and put down inside a loaf and a pitcher of milk. She heard a rustling beside her and sensed the girl's fear. "Don't be afraid," she said softly, "You are safe for tonight, but see that you are away before first light. God be with you."

She locked herself inside the house, and waited long for sleep.

In the morning the pitcher was empty and the girl had gone.

Thursday October 21ˢᵗ

Araminta and Laetitia walked down the beech avenue to the lake. They carried a basket full of pieces of bread for the ducks and moorhens. The sun was shining across the park; the grass near the path was striped with white bands where the tree trunks had protected the overnight frost from the sun.

Araminta had awoken in a much happier frame of mind than she had gone to bed. Her fears of developing a chill that would ruin her ball by weeping eyes and red nose proved groundless. The cheerful sunshine and her appearance in the full-length looking glass as Celestine moved busily around her on her knees, a measure around her neck and her mouth full of pins, had afforded her enough pleasure to thrust her more serious worries back into the shadowy recesses of her mind.

Breakfast, however, had not been an entirely comfortable meal. Lady Fenborough, making an unaccustomed appearance at table, was brought a letter. She cut it open and read it in silence, with a tightening of her lips. She thrust it across the table to her husband. "It is too tiresome, Edward. Yet I suppose we have no choice but to receive them as hospitably as we can."

Lord Fenborough read the letter through before he replied. He carefully refolded the missive and handed it back to his wife.

"But of course, my dear, if your mother wishes to be with us we shall be delighted to entertain her. I see she intends arriving today: you will have to speak to Cairns. We shall have so many guests that one or two extra are of no consequence."

"But you know how she"- Lady Fenborough bit her lip, "always finds travelling in the cold weather so irksome. But indeed, it is a beautiful day today for the season, so all may be well."

Araminta wondered what her hostess had intended to say, and was interested as Frederick, on his way to replenish his plate from the side board paused behind her to explain, sotto voce, "My grandmother has just invited herself for a visit. It is without doubt the prospect of the ball which has brought her – matchmaking attracts her as the candle the moth. She is convinced that my dear mama has an insufficient grasp of the intrigues which are essential to the art."

"It is only to be expected," – It was impossible to tell whether Lord Fenborough had heard his son's words or not – "that she would be interested to attend a ball at which so many of her grandchildren will be present. I see from her letter that she made arrangements as soon as she heard of our planned diversion."

"How many will there be at the ball, Papa?"

"Some thirty couples, I expect, for the dancing, apart from those who prefer the pleasure of cards or conversation."

"Thirty couples!" Araminta was a little daunted by the size of the party, so very few of whom she knew, for in her own neighbourhood rarely more than a dozen couples stood up, and most of those she had known from childhood. She wondered about Laetitia's grandmother and why she was so formidable that the anticipation of her arrival could so perturb her daughter; for since the letter had come she had eaten little but cut and recut the bread upon her plate meeting nobody's eye, until she rose abruptly, said to her husband, "You are quite right I must see Cairns at once to make arrangements," and left the room in dignified haste. He half rose as if to follow her, then turned politely to the girls.

"Are you planning to walk abroad this fine morning?"

"Indeed we are, Papa. It must be at least two weeks since I last fed the ducks, so we intend to go down to the lake with a bag of morsels for them. Now it is getting colder there will be ice on the lake and they will be ready for what we have to give them."

"Useful things, ducks. You girls feed them, we shoot them and then they feed us."

"Do not forget we sleep on them too, some of us until far in the morning," William reminded his friend who had arrived late at the table."

Then his Lordship picked up the paper, and the young men strolled out towards the stables. The girls collected a suitable bag of scraps from the housekeeper

and set out . They were both glad to be away from the constraints of the meal.

They leaned over the parapet of the bridge, which was carved with an elegant balustrade. This spanned the shallow canal which slid in a smooth line in front of them, over a weir into the ornamental lake.

"And you say that all this was dug out by your grandfather's workmen! What a task that must have been. And it all looks so natural, as if it was always there. Look, there is a pair of swans by that little island, and now here come the mallards."

As she watched the ducks converge beneath them and skid to a halt in a flurry of spray and feathers she wondered if they all belonged to the lake, or if some had come from further afield, perhaps even from the stream that ran through the village at home or the wild tarn among the rocks behind her house. How long would it take them? How wonderful to have wings and come and go at will. They certainly looked the same as the birds at home as they squabbled and rammed one another to get at the scraps. She laughed aloud as one large, pompous drake had the crust to which he was just inclining his beak snatched away by a busy little moorhen who had been biding her time at a discreet distance. She leaned out over the balustrade to throw some larger pieces to the better-mannered or more timid birds that were waiting at the edge of the jostling mob.

Suddenly Laetitia began to speak, quietly and urgently, her eyes still on the greedy birds, her hands still throwing out scraps. "Araminta, has your mama ever suggested marriage to you? Or spoken to you of it all?"

"I recall that when Marianne was married, over a year ago, I told Mama I had no wish to marry, because I did not wish to have to be sensible all the time, and have to take care of a household and children, and she smiled and told me that showed I was not yet ready to become a wife. She said it would be time enough to talk of marriage when I wanted my own home and husband and indeed, it seems to me that perhaps, in three or four years … when I have met someone I could love and live with – but not yet. I mean to be free for a while yet."

"But mine has to me." Laetitia, busy with her own thoughts had not heard all her friend had said, "She has to me, and I am so frightened. Of course it would be exciting to be the mistress of a house, and have nobody to tell you what gowns to wear, and to keep as many little dogs as you wanted, and to be able to order just what you wanted every day for dinner - and from what I have seen he seems a pleasant enough young man – and he will certainly be very rich and his family is quite as good as ours, and if both Mama and Papa wish it – and I now see so little of Frederick that for him I might as well not be here – but oh Minta, what will it be to be a wife! And besides his ears stick out and he talks so quick I cannot always hear what he is saying."

"Whom do you mean? Are you talking about someone I've met? Somebody who will be at the ball? Ears that stick out and a quick way of talking… Can you – could you – be talking about William?"

Laetitia looked away, but blushed and nodded. Araminta was abashed at the thought that marriage - a real life, for ever marriage with a household and even children of her own – should be coming so close to one of her own age, who only a few months before had had her head full of highwaymen and swarthy admirers.

"And how do you feel about him yourself? Surely you cannot take a man in marriage just to oblige your parents. It is you, not they, who will have to live with him for the rest of your life. Is he so thoroughly amiable in yours eyes that you can care for him as you should? I suppose," (very quietly) "your mama will speak to you before the wedding and explain to you all you need to know. Marianne tells me Mama spoke to her in that way, and it gave her courage."

"How old was your sister?"

"She was eighteen, but she had known Edgar for four years, and our families were always together. If it was me, I would not think I knew the young man well enough… There are so many things I would want to know about any young man before I would wed him, you may be sure. He is certainly nothing like the young heroes and dashing officers we dwelt on in our schooldays, but then we were children."

Letty was making up her mind to further confidences. "It is not just that Mama spoke to me yesterday evening and asked if I would be willing to take him if he made me an offer but… this morning, as I was coming out of my room, Frederick was waiting for me. He caught me around the waist and kissed me like he used to. Then he said, 'Will you do something for your big brother, puss? Something really important?' I could only nod. ' 'Tis a great deal to ask, but I think my little sister is truly fond of me and would like to help me, would she not? I believe that my friend William is likely to make you an offer of marriage at the ball. Now, do not blush and turn your head away, Letty. You are a pretty girl, and the young men will be flocking round you like flies to a honey pot. If he is your first admirer I am surprised. Now please, Letty dear, for my sake, please do accept him, there's a love.' I stammered out,' Why Frederick, are you so eager to be rid of me?' and he replied, 'Why as for that, I am at his house as often as I am here, if not more, so we would still see just as much of each other, so that would be pleasant, would it not? But there are various reasons you will just have to trust me for. It will be very hard for me if you are such a heartless girl as to refuse him.' Then he kissed me again, very lovingly, and ran on downstairs."

"He had no right to speak to you like that!. You must follow your own heart in this… What do you really feel about him?"

"He is all the world – oh you mean William. I know nothing evil of him, and I dare say I could come to like him very well in time. I suppose if he wants me to take him I shall. I have always done what he wanted, ever since I was five years old."

"But you are not five years old now!" The words leapt out, but it seemed Letty had not heard them. A silence fell between the girls, deep and for the moment unbridgeable.

Then they heard a distant rumble of wheels and saw a gleaming carriage, drawn by four horses and supported behind by two footmen run along the drive and pull up before the main doors of the hall.

"That is Grandmamma arriving now."

"Should we return to the house, so you can bid her

welcome and we can help entertain her?"

"By no means. Grandmamma is close on sixty, and does not wish to be seen except at such times as she determines. She will retire immediately with her maid and hairdresser and we shall see nothing of her until teatime."

"What kind of person is she? And is your grandfather with her?"

"Oh no, he died many years ago. He had a fall out hunting and broke his neck."

"Fortunately for Grandmamma." Frederick and his friend had come down to the lake with fishing rods, and while William made a cast in the lake well downstream from the flocking birds Frederick had come up to talk to the girls. He pushed himself between them, leaning one arm on the parapet, the other on his sister's shoulder

"You carry on cramming these overweight fowls with bread, while I feed your friend with gossip about our relations. Grandmamma is a highly ambitious lady, who sees no reason why her grandchildren should not succeed as well as she has done, eh, puss?"

Laetitia looked unhappy. "Oh please. Do not talk like that."

Frederick stroked her shoulder affectionately. "You're too sweet to be real, puss. Sometimes I think you must be made of icing sugar." He nibbled at her fingers. "Yes, definitely. Take care you are never caught out in a shower. Well, Araminta, when you are duly presented to my ancestress, do not be deceived by her manner into wondering of which earl she is the daughter. You must not let her see that you know, but her father was neither more nor less than an attorney!"

"He had an extensive and highly lucrative practice in York, a shrewd wife, and one very pretty daughter. Oh yes and no sons, which is very much to the point. He took his beautiful daughter everywhere, to the theatre and the assembly rooms, baiting his hook with her as deftly as William there and threw her into society to catch land and a title for him. Nor had he long to wait. She was no more than fifteen when honest Sir John Hastings cast his eyes upon her at a concert. Now her parents saw that young Laetitia (for our Letty is named for her) had charmed that forty year old baronet. So when he next called on business at the house he was invited to the drawing room for a glass of wine en famille, with Laetitia in her best white lace and ribbons, and within a few weeks the fine, fat trout was offering up his house, name and broad acres to the captivating attorney's daughter.

"But 'twas well for her that he did not live above ten more years before snapping his neck like a stick of celery, for this gave her the disposal of her children, and she set up her ambuscades with her daughter Elizabeth, who was also considered a most attractive young woman, one in whom favourable face and fortune were united to an uncommon degree. The old lady stayed with her tried and tested hunting grounds, and it was at one of Mr Hebden's concerts in the Assembly Rooms that the two of them hauled in their fine catch, for Papa, being the second lord and with an estate to match was far above their reasonable expectations. And so she has come down now to supervise this night's sport."

"Perhaps, sir, she also keeps watch for pike and such, that would snatch at the bait and escape capture."

"I can see you are an expert angler. Miss Minta,. Indeed she will, and there will be many a pike keeping watch in his brocade waistcoat tomorrow night. She will be well in her element, for as well as her little namesake here there will be half a dozen other grandchildren for her to bait her hooks with."

"I do wish that you and Letty would tell me something of who is expected at the ball. How many will be staying at the hall, and will they all be your cousins? Are any of the neighbouring families coming?"

"We shall be not quite putting up the whole sixty, but there will be a good number lodged here. While you two have been throwing out the bread and the greedy fowl have crowded to the spot, eager to miss nothing they may grab or find on offer, the flower of the county and cousinage have, more leisurely, begun to pack themselves into chaises and coaches to converge upon our ballroom with the same intent. But ask Letty about them; all this talk of angling has reminded me I have a fine fish awaiting down below."

He left them and in a few moments was adjusting his tackle by his friend. The bread was finished, the sky was becoming overcast, and Letty proposed they walk in the warmth of the aviary.

While the girls were feeding the ducks and talking, Betty was preparing gruel for her grandmother, stirring the pan on the hob. She had found an old doll for Nell and wrapped it in a shawl, and the little girl was sitting under the table, rocking the doll back and forth, singing it an interminable, wordless song. There was no other sound in the room except the crackling of the fire. Betty looked across to where Mrs Brownrigg rested propped on the pillow. Her hand lay on the bedspread. All her life Betty had known her grandmother's firm red hand – sewing, stroking, slapping, stirring, shovelling – and was troubled to see it now blotched, greyish and almost still. But her eyes in the sunken face were alert and interested, watching Betty's every move as she leaned over the pan of gruel.

"Fifteen years gone I was standing where you are now, and she were laying where I am now. And that was when I knew she was going, and her so troubled in her spirit and restless. Aye, we found her in the byre, too, one dark night."

Betty turned to the old lady. "So you were waking last night, then."

She laughed. "And many a night, my dear. I don't seem somehow to have much need of sleep now – maybe because I'm going to sleep long soon enough. Oh I heard. Joseph's a good lad. He faced them out right enough. If your John grows into as good a man he'll do well for you.. Yes, it put me in mind of her, the other one. Fifteen years ago and you little but a baby. I went out to see to the beasts, and there she was in the straw, tossing and turning with the fever. Joseph and my Thomas carried her in and we laid her in this very bed. I thought from the start she might be sinking, but we hoped that with care and good food - but 'twas not to be. But we did what we could for her."

"But who was she? And why were you looking after her?"

"Look out for that pan! You'll have it over. Well, when we brought her in we could see she was quite a young woman, and she had once been well favoured. But now she was haggard and sick, and had long lost any spirit she may have had. I nursed her for seven days until she died."

"And did you never find out anything about her? Did she die a stranger?"

"She never would tell me her name. But in her fever she said – oh, such things, things she like as not would never have told her in her right mind."

She relapsed into silence. A late fly buzzed in the sun on the window pane.

"Some of it I can recall to this day. 'Twas a day just like this, the sun was lying across the hearth in just the same way, so I could hardly see her face, and she twisted and turned under the covers. 'They've all gone, all gone on and left me, all gone and he has left me too' she was muttering again and again. And then she would start up and call out, 'What time is it? I cannot hear them on the stage, I've missed my cue. Oh God, I should be on now, and I've missed my cue. What can I do? I should be on, and they have missed me.' Then I remembered that there had been a band of travelling actors giving a play in a barn down in Pateley the week before – not that we had gone, for we have neither time nor inclination for such godless mockeries as people pretending to be what they are not, and speaking lewdly to one another in company – and I bethought me she might have been with them. Then a neighbour who had been to the play came in, and she recognised her. She said she had acted the part of a beautiful but cruel woman who had a most fair and virtuous step-daughter, and she tried all her arts to keep the young woman apart from the young man she truly loved. She said she had looked very elegant, in a blue and silver gown. But in truth, her clothes were poor enough and she had the look of hunger upon her. One day the company was playing and the next day they were gone. But they must have left her and her husband behind because she was sick, and they had no way to take a sick person with them. Indeed, when I saw her next, my neighbour told me they had left behind another sick man over Stukely way. And his wife stayed with him."

"But what happened to your sick woman's husband? Why was he not with her when you found her in the byre?"

"That I do not know. It seems he just abandoned her to her fate. Maybe he was afraid her sickness might infect him. Perhaps he rejoined his friends in the company, or found himself some other work. Or perhaps we are unjust to his memory, and he went to seek help and perished by some accident."

"No wonder the poor woman was so distressed."

"No indeed. But that was not all that was troubling her. There was something else... something that she believed only she knew and she was fearful lest the knowledge should die with her."

"So she told you?"

"She told me, and I have never spoken of it to a soul. I

do not know if she spoke true, and even if she did there was naught that such as I could do to remedy it….. and yet, now I am coming to her case, I know why she had to speak. I am not sure."

The sick woman looked and sounded more uncertain than Betty would have thought possible for her confident, sensible grandmother. Her wasted hand trembled and touched her lips.

Betty leaned over her and took her hand. "If, if you would feel easier by passing on to me that which she said, grandmother, I will listen to it. I think I can keep quiet. If you wish it, I will promise never to speak of it myself."

"Nay, my dear, do not bind yourself to silence. The time may come when you know it is right for you to speak out, as it never has for me. 'Tis foolish, I know, but I feel as if I would fail that poor woman if her tale died with me. Is the child listening?"

Betty looked at Nell, now fast asleep under the table, and carried her, still clutching the doll, to a settle on the far side of the room. She tucked her in with a blanket, then crossed the room to the bed, and took her grandmother's hand again.

"She is sound asleep, but even if she wakes she will not hear us if we speak low. Besides, she is still too young to understand a great deal of what is said."

"And that is why you must never talk secrets in the hearing of so young a child, a little child may well do great harm by repeating, in all innocence, that which it does not understand to those who should not hear it. I wonder if I should ….. no, I cannot shake her off, I feel it as a debt I must pay before I am free to go... But, Betty, she had not always been a player. She had been a private attendant of a young lady in her youth. Some seven years before, her mistress had married. Her husband brought his bride home at Christmas. There was feasting, for he loved her dearly, and it was a fine match for her. She was very young and, it seemed to her maid, cared more for his land and position than his person, pushed into the marriage perhaps by her widowed mother. Well, her husband was a Member of Parliament, and his duties called him away to London in mid-January. He did not return until well into April. His son and heir was born at the end of November, a seven months' child, as it is said. But this woman says she delivered the baby, and a healthier full-term infant she says she never beheld, and since then she had herself borne and buried five. The baby was born on a Friday, with only herself in attendance. Her mistress had refused to let her call a midwife.

"On Monday her mistress's mother arrived and definitely pronounced it a seven months' child, saying that most of the women in her family found it fell out so with their firstborn. Then she rid herself of the maid. She told me she remembered every detail as if it was yesterday, how the woman caused a valuable brooch to be placed among her things, then reported its loss and insisted on searching the belongings of all the servants. The poor woman said she was never so astonished as when her bundle was unwrapped and the brooch fell out.

"She was then locked in her room to await the constable,

and the gallows, but she escaped by the window and ran away in the night, taking only the clothes she stood up in. There was a great hue and cry after her, but she made her escape, travelling by night and resting in disused barns by day, taking what food she could, for she durst not enter a shop for fear of being taken up – and who would believe her word against a great lady?

"When she was exhausted and desperate for food – for she had never before had to shift for herself – she fell in with this group of players. She fell desperately sick of a fever, and was out of her mind for a few days. One of their number had just died in childbed and they needed another woman to join their company, so cared for her and pressed her to join them as she recovered. It would have been hard to refuse, for the reward for her capture was tempting to such poor people, and it was only because she could be of use to them that they did not betray her. And I fear she wed her man under similar compulsion, for she spoke of him with fear and disgust. At first when she appeared upon the stage she took pains to disguise her face, but as time went on she felt this was no longer necessary. She found she could learn her lines with more ease than many, and being able to write and a good reader was soon of value to the company. She was popular with the people who came to the plays, for she spoke loud enough to be heard, and, she said, could look queenly when the play required it, but she always in her heart despised her work, and hated the necessity which had brought her to it, and gave her such low companions. 'Sometimes,' she told me, ' I almost forget my past life, or it seems like a dream of splendour among the dirty straw and coarse food, but the remembrance of that time comes back most bitterly when we travel in these parts. And once I saw the lad himself, with the man who deemed himself his father, and I thought, "Aha, Lord Fenborough! What a blow I could deal you if I was so minded!" And yet that is mere foolishness, for if I could not win a hearing as a lady's maid, how could I as a poor dirty player ?" ' "

Betty exclaimed, and her grandmother was startled. "Oh I did not think to let the name fall in that way. But it is heavy on my mind, and the more so for the young man is almost of age. I am very pleased you are no longer in the service of that house, for evil will come of evil, but then, if we knew all, who knows but that most of the great families of the realm have been at some time in like case. Sin may wear satin slippers as well as clogs. But if the tale be true, I would not like to be either the young man's mother or her mother, when they come to lie as I do and look back over the years of their life." Her voice died away, and she leaned back, exhausted.

Betty kissed her, "But I am sure you can only look back over hundreds of good memories, grandmother. Try some of this gruel I have made and then sleep for a while, and then perhaps you can tell me some of your own happier memories that you would like me to share. I would like to know more about my mother when she was little Nellie's age. And I like to hear about how you met grandfather when you were in service and only fourteen years old."

Soon the old woman was peacefully asleep. The square of sunlight from the window moved gently over the stone floor. Betty sat by the fire spinning. Old woman and infant asleep, and a girl quietly spinning. An observer would have seen her, with her deft, repetitive movements and the humming of the wheel, as a perfect image of peace, for he could not see the noise and turmoil behind her serious gaze.

Thursday evening

My dearest Louisa,

It is going to be such a great ball – thirty couple in all! There is to be a great number of guests staying in the house. Several of them have arrived already. We saw from the grounds the arrival of Laetitia's maternal grandmother in a splendid coach, with two powdered footmen, but I did not meet her until we took tea in the drawing-room

She is very upright in carriage, not tall but with her head dressed high, and her waist appears smaller than mine. She was in a magnificent gown of dark green silk with many bows and ruchings and a great quantity of delicate cream lace. Her eyes are dark and very piercing for a lady of her age. She is very old, nearly sixty. Letty says. She has a long pointed nose, and a very small mouth. You can tell by the set of her mouth and chin that she is not accustomed to being thwarted. She was considered a very great beauty as a girl, and the portrait of her done for her wedding – at the age of fifteen! Scarce a year older than you! – shows she was very handsome and confident. Indeed, you can still see that she was a beauty, and I noticed she can command the attention of the whole room when she speaks.

When I was introduced to her, she asked me if I had stayed at Muncaster, and if I was on visiting terms with several noble families of whom I had but heard, and on hearing that I was not, paid me no more attention than bare civility to her host's guests required. I fancy I detected a flicker of relief cross her face as she scrutinised me through her glass, and suppose she has decided that I am not a sufficient temptation to lead any of her grandchildren to forsake a decent mercenary prudence! You will understand that I entertain no more warmth towards her than she towards me, but I too have learnt civility and know how to conduct myself with decent courtesy to one so much my senior. Although I do not like her, I can but admire her determination; in a more barbarous age I could well see her acting as Macbeth's wife did in the play – but she would not have spoiled everything at the close!

I admit to more curiosity about the six cousins who are coming to stay; Laetitia's Aunt Alice and Uncle Thomas are coming with their sons Edward and Henry (who are both a little older than Frederick, and their daughters Elizabeth, who is my age, and Margaret, who is fifteen.) Then there are John and James, twins aged nineteen, who are the sons of her Uncle Edward. I forget the name of his wife. Letty's other aunt, Aunt Margaret, who was here when we came, will not be returning, for her child is due next month, and the three others are too young to be brought to a ball. I asked Letty to tell me what they were all like, and she said she could do better than that.

Then she took me into the music room, and bade me look up at the painted ceiling. It was a pastoral scene crowded with nymphs and shepherdessess, with shepherds serenading Apollo's statue, a pretty subject for a music room. Letty told me to look closely and see if I recognised anyone. At first all was a riot of draperies, verdure and fleecy lambs, but when I looked closely at one of the lambs I saw it was more like a little white dog than a lamb –

indeed, it was Laura! And the shepherdess who was hanging a garland of roses round her neck was the image of Letty herself – as to face, for I would never expect to see her hair flowing and her bosom bare were she standing upon the floor rather than floating upon the ceiling of the music room! Then I saw that the hunter transfixing a fine stag was Frederick in a spotted lion skin, and the statue of Apollo had Lord Fenborough's features. Lady Fenborough was more difficult to find, for I consider the painter had made her features more classic and beautiful than they are in the flesh, but after a while I realised she was depicted as the Goddess Venus who was smiling down upon the scene.

The Letty told me that the picture had been done about two years before and many of the members of the family, who had been staying there were included. I noticed Aunt Margaret as an attendant upon the altar holding a taper. Letty pointed out to me those whom I had not met. Seated upon a mossy bank, gazing up at Venus, with plume and parchment in hand as a poet receiving celestial inspiration was Uncle Charles. I will not be seeing him. It seems he would have liked to become a lawyer, but his mother would not hear of it and insisted on him entering the church if he must have a profession. He is now a canon of Christ Church Oxford, until such time as his mother succeeds in intriguing him into a bishopric. Cousins Elizabeth and Margaret were weaving garlands of flowers to welcome Venus (or perhaps to deck the altar, I could not decide which), while Edward and Henry were playing shepherd pipes

Edward especially looks most handsome, with flowing brown locks and a fine, bold eye, but then the painter has represented Frederick with the aspect of a young god, which he has not, and completely left out the pimples on his chin. The twins are tending their flocks in the middle distance, and casting languishing looks at two nymphs whom Letty could not identify, while Aunt Margaret's small children are little putti flying about Venus. When I looked carefully at the landskip behind I could discern the ruins of the Abbey and (with a shudder) the stone circle and the figure of the Druid. I wish it had not been there, I had forgot him. But I shall do my practising now worse than ever, with one eye on the ceiling. Is it not a delightful way to portray the members of a family? I do wish some artist would paint me in the midst of our family, and that artist to be as indulgent towards all our features as that painter towards Letty's family.

I was a little disconcerted this afternoon. Letty was closeted with her mother and dressmaker so I walked alone in the aviary where I could never tire of watching the pretty parakeets.

As I was trying to pick out the new arrivals among the busy little flock darting to and fro in the branches I heard the sound of a large dog approaching and turned round to be almost overwhelmed by William's bloodhound, Prince, which leapt up scrabbling with his paws on my bodice and licking my neck. He was so like Uncle Jeremy's bloodhounds at home that I seized him by the front paws, shook them, then, rubbing his back in the way they like so, talked to him as I would to one of ours.

Then I realised William was behind him, calling him away, apologising and begging me not to be alarmed, for he should not hurt me. "I should think not!" I told him. "He wants to play, don't you then, Prince?" And so William and I fell into conversation. He said he had expected a young lady to be frightened by such a large dog "so unlike that little pet dog of your friend's – Lily or some such name". I did not mean to be disloyal to Letty, but as I rubbed Prince's hair I told him my preference was for a real dog, for Laura (though undoubtedly pretty and good tempered) seems to me to be more of a toy than a real animal. And I told him about the bloodhounds at home, and how Uncle Jeremy was hoping to breed a champion from his prize bitch, and how we had just found a suitable dog we hoped would oblige us all. He laughed and said he never thought young ladies to be concerned in such matters – and I suddenly felt ashamed, and blushed, and I told him I was sorry if I had said aught amiss, and I hoped he would put it down to Prince's fault, as he reminded me of home and all my acquaintance there, and so had led me speak to him as if he was a friend I had known for years and then – oh dear, Louisa, it made me so uncomfortable – he looked directly at me and said he only wished he had known me for so long and he hoped we would indeed become better acquainted.

"For indeed, " he added, as if to himself, "my tongue and teeth get all tangled when every word I say is to be suitable for a delicate ear and a pink and white sensibility." I gave no indication I had heard his, yet it did not quite please me. Then he asked me for the first two dances tomorrow!

And I was so confused, and pleased! But I am afraid Letty will not like it, but surely I cannot be expected to refuse. I only hope I am asked again, perhaps by the handsome Edward, so that I can tell him I am engaged, but will give him the next two. Then we were both rather awkward, and I asked him about his day's sport, and he recalled that he was on his way to the gun room and should not keep Frederick waiting. "I only came in here," said he, "because Prince had dashed in before me, but I am glad I did." Then he was gone.

Dear, dearest Louisa, who knows the secrets of my heart, you will know that never before has anyone spoken so to me – there was little enough, and I am so agitated. I do not like him so well as all that and besides, there is another thing, a secret concerning another I may not tell you of, that is confusing and makes it difficult to know how to conduct myself. But it is a great thing to know that one, not partial like a cousin, should notice and prefer – for my glass tells me what I would own to none but you, that there are many young women more beautiful - indeed, you yourself will be one such. I am now the more looking forward to tomorrow night. I trust the letter I shall write on Saturday will not completely wear you out. If only I could write all that I wish to say to you the post horse would be lodged in mud to his belly with the weight of news!

My dearest love to you all
Araminta

P.S. Aunt Alice and her family have just arrived. The painter omitted a quite marked cast in Edward's eye, but Henry is a mighty pleasant young man. Elizabeth seems much more accomplished and at ease in grand company than I am, even Margaret can smile and flicker her fan in a way I never thought to at her age. I am very glad I have a partner to start the ball with, though I still feel shy to tell Letty lest she should feel slighted.

Celestine wrote that day in her journal

Friday October 22nd

This is likely to be a most busy day for us all, but I have risen well before dawn to set down the events of last night, for fear I should come to think them but a dream, or to suppose that horror had turned my brain...

Well, the house is full of guests with their various maids and valets. For the first time since I have been here, the house seemed fully alive last night. I could fancy that, whatever the secret wishes of its lady might be, the rooms themselves are downright glad of occupation, with blazing fires, and covers removed, and candles in dark places. One of the ground floor rooms at the back has been set aside for meals for the personal attendants, with a small sitting room leading off it.

And indeed, having set eyes upon Lady Hastings' maid Millicent I can only wonder that ladies' maids have not been allotted a room at the front of the house. She was in finer silk than many a lady I have seen, and her glances and gestures betoken an ineffable superiority. Lady Fenborough herself has not half her arrogance and sense of dignity. Yet I must admit that she, her mistress and her hairdresser (a willowy young man with a languidly curled wig and fingers like melting tapers) are in their way artists. I would say that God and Millicent alone know what the old lady truly looks like, and I suspect that her discretion is as great as her artistry. The only visible part of Lady Hastings which is not created in her closet is her sharp little eyes; I have seen the like sometimes on traders who never stray from their vocation to extract the maximum profit from every transaction. I suspect not a word passes her lips without calculation, and every movement of her fan is planned. It was amusing (though it made me angry) to observe her relief as she scrutinised my young mistress and decided she presented no matrimonial shoals or quick sands for her grandsons. My young lady may not have the finance behind her or the elegance of figure to please Her Ladyship, but she is worth all her grandchildren put together.

Leonie is, as one might expect, most hostile towards Millicent; she appeared tonight with more variety of lace than I have ever seen before except at a draper's counter and her head more elaborately dressed than is her wont. Each lady's maid treats the other with chilly courtesy and the rest of us are caught in the cold blast. After one embrace so frosty we could almost see the icicles forming on their elbows, they took the easy chairs and proceeded to amuse themselves by pointing out to each other, not inaudibly, the rural simplicities of the hair and attire of the rest of us. More than one poor girl was in tears. I, however, have some sympathy for the haughty pair. Whether I would sooner serve the imperious old lady or the vacillating middle-aged one I am not sure; indeed, I feel that I would not myself tolerate service with either.

When I was first at my lady's, I used sometimes to take corn to the hens in the run behind the kitchen garden, and I noticed that the one with the coldest eye and the least charity to her weaker and younger sisters was not the finest, but the second best fowl, who in this way made up for the humiliation she endured at the behest of her superior. Our small sitting-room makes a fine hen run.

As most of the others present knew one another, I was perforce a listener to much of the conversation. On my right:

"….. such quantities of delicate snowy lace, my dear…"

"I admire Lady Hastings' taste vastly, and how sensible of her to be swathed completely to the chin, for nothing reveals the years like the base of the neck. Now we have been looking at hair ornaments in the Chinese style –"

"Yes, I had gathered your mistress has acquired a taste for the exotic. Your dressmaking skills have recently been much employed on a jacket for an ape, I believe?"

"A most fascinating little creature!"

"My lady would have its neck wrung for vermin."

"Perhaps its wrinkled brow and skinny hand disturb her in some way."

I would not wish to intervene in that contest. On my left:

"I am so glad we two are to lie together. I do not greatly care for the attic storey here at night."

"But there has been good fires lit."

"No it is not that." The speaker, a pretty young woman in her late teens, lowered her voice. "It is the sense of something … untoward about the place. I felt it last time and now, after all that has happened –"

"Aha, the slain druid! Are you afraid then that he will creep up behind you and place an icy hand upon your neck?"

The young woman shrieked as the speaker suited the action to the word.

"Frank! Go away! I declare I shall not sleep a wink."

"Indeed, I was talking to the girl who came to tend the fire in our apartment," said Phoebe, the maid of Lady Fenborough's sister, "and she seemed to be in a state of great excitement. She was muttering about the phantom of a monk with a candle gliding along the corridors"

"Had he his head under his arm? Life must be dull for the servants here if they have to invent such ghostly tales to keep themselves amused."

It would not be long before the two younger women were ready to see anything in a shadowy corner. I was not surprised that Phoebe asked Frank to fetch some more candles.

I see I have not yet come to the meat of my story. I am tarrying in the sitting-room like one reluctant to leave the warmth of the fire to venture out into the cold night air; I am reluctant to leave the safety of the stuffy room and the gossip in order to think again of what followed. But time is getting short.

I decided to retire to our room. I had some final details to add to the gown I had been making, and a growing determination that Araminta should be turned out in a way to compel admiration and give the old lady a pang of uneasiness. Besides, the wine had been good and I had perhaps taken more than I was accustomed to – for what reason I left that secure, if unfriendly, room I do not know, but I took up a candlestick and slipped away unnoticed.

As I stood on the landing near our room, shielding the candle's flame from the draught that blew down the dark corridor, I saw a figure descending the other staircase. It was approaching the level at which I stood: it carried a lantern so the face should have been visible, but a cowl was pulled low over the front of the head. The left hand was shielding the flame, which shone red through it. The figure was wrapped in a long, loose robe of dark stuff, and was moving in silence.

My first thought, I am amazed to recall, was fascination. Who has not wondered in her own heart if phantoms really exist? And if they do, who would not want to see for herself? Ere I well knew what I was doing, I had darted into our apartment and wrapped myself in my cloak, kicking off my high heeled shoes and replacing them with slippers in which I, too, could move silently.

Then I blew out the candle and followed the shape. By the time I reached the staircase it was out of sight, but a yellow glow showed it to be ahead, round the next bend in the staircase. I followed, taking care to keep well in the shadows, still – as I am now – unable to decide whether it were human or not. A phantom should not require a lantern, I know, but it might still choose to carry one.

When it slipped out into the courtyard I could not bear to lose it and followed as best I could. I can see quite well in the dark and the moon, though not yet risen, was throwing a faint light from below the horizon.

As I expected, the form made its way towards the abbey. When it reached the wall surrounding the ruins it pushed at the ivy and passed through. I was now watching from beneath a knot of dark trees: I durst go no closer. I still had not seen the face. I saw the figure set down the lantern, and remove a stone from beneath one of the pointed windows, through which wisps of cloud and a few bright stars could be seen. I could not watch what he did, for his back was between me and his light, but I marked the exact position of the stone. I will not set it down here. Then as I watched, one of the faintly visible pillars seemed to shiver, and move towards the window. The phantom I had been following picked up its lantern and turned round, and I saw a second cowled figure approach. They met, and went out together into the depths of the abbey through one of the arched doorways.

And then, when they were gone, the terror that had been so strangely held back by curiosity fell upon me. I was afraid I had seen two supernatural visitants, and equally afraid that I had not. How could I have for a moment forgotten that other night, with the dead body in the moonlight, and how my young mistress had seen the ghostly monk? Dead or living, those two in the abbey shrank me with fear.

I must have turned and fled, for the next I knew I was stumbling across the courtyard. Making for the door I saw one come across from the stable - yard Porrott. He heard me, and held up his light. He exclaimed seeing me – as I suppose – pale and trembling, and drew me into the warmth of the kitchen, where work had ceased for the night. He sat me down before the dying fire and brought me wine. I had intended to tell no-one what I had seen but perhaps from relief – or the wine – I told him the whole story.

He was not inclined to credit any supernatural visitations and seemed almost angry at my hardihood, and I was too shaken to resent his speaking to me more roughly than any man had done since I was a child. He told me he would teach me how to handle a pistol if I insisted on such foolish behaviour and – I have not the time to set down all he said, even if I could recall it. He did not speak of his own plans, but I think that at some time today he will visit the abbey.

I wonder if I spoke foolishly, for I cannot put out of my mind that he and the mysterious monk are much of a height. True, the monk walks like an old man, but such a gait would not be difficult to assume. Surely, if it were he, he would not pour scorn on my superstitious fears – unless he were a very subtle man, which I think he may be. When he offers to show me how to shoot straight I shall not accept his offer; commit myself alone with a gun to one I know so little, with one violent death already!

By mid-morning the kitchen was full of heat and bustle. Huge flames leapt up the chimney, throwing shadows and orange flickers upon the wall, for the day was overcast. The biggest shadows swaying and rolling on the back wall belonged to the smallest people in the room, the two black pages. They were crouched upon the hearth rug, playing with Jacko. The chain on his waist was firmly attached to a leather strap around the wrist of one of them, and the cook had threatened to chase them all out of the kitchen if "that heathen-looking creature gets loose among my pots and pans."

As she rubbed the butter into her pastry at the central wooden table she glanced at them indulgently. They were a beautiful pair, and her heart yearned at the thought of such little children being snatched from their mother. No-one was sure of their age, but they could not be older than six or seven. They were usually silent with everyone except each other; when they had first entered the household they understood little English and they still often found it convenient to conceal how much they could understand. They spoke to each other in whispers, in their own language made up of rags and tatters of all the tongues they had heard. If they knew their own names they did not tell them, responding obediently enough to whatever it pleased those around them. They were identical twins and had never been parted; each was the other's security and love. They liked the kitchen, which gave them warmth, food and casual kindness, but they took good care never to admit to their hearts those they cajoled for titbits and smiled at so delightfully. They had learnt early to trust none but themselves.

When they had been handed Jacko to look after that morning they had wordlessly agreed he should be admitted to their fellowship. This excitable chained little stranger gave them something to protect and teach for the first time in their lives. Now they were telling him about the plans they had made; how, when they were men, they would steal one of the gleaming guns, take one of the best horses and ride off to the sea. Then they would get into a boat and sail back to the place they came from with its blue sky and hot-smelling dust. They would walk straight into the big shady house and kill all the people there, then throw open the doors and invite everyone in for a feast. They would be the kings then, and sit on big gold chairs, and have servants, and always eat what they wanted, and wear laced coats all the time, and play all day long and never have to stand still in the drawing-room beside my lady, and it would never rain or be foggy. And they promised Jacko he would be with them, because they would steal him too.

They quietly let out his chain so that he could grab a handful of raisins from the jar on the table, tugged him back, tickled him, and all rolled over in a giggling heap.

Celestine had to step carefully round them as she heated her irons at the fireside. She was in the kitchen by the cook's courtesy as ironing was so much easier with a really hot fire close at hand. She had put herself and the fine silk gown she was pressing in a shady corner well out of the way of waving ladles and floury hands. Concerned as she was to bring out the material to its best advantage, and particularly intent on detail as one can be after a night of inadequate sleep, she did not hear the door open as Betty entered.

Sarah, who was scrubbing out a wooden bucket turned at the sound and ran over to her.

"Betty, my dear! Whatever are you doing here? Has your father thought on and sent you back to work with us again? Or have you come to help us tonight with the great ball we are having? Let me take your shawl, and sit down to warm yourself at the fire, do."

Betty hugged her friend, but spoke first to the cook. "I hope you won't object to the liberty, Mrs Sanderson, but I have been visiting my poor auntie in the village and I have some time to wait for John, so Mother said I could come along to see you all."

"I won't deny it's pleasant to see you, Betty, but there's no idle hands in my kitchen today. If you are minded to stay a while, there's a basket of peas for shelling just come in from the garden. Sarah, you may go and help her, for you will have a deal to say to one another, girls is always the same, clack-clacking together like a pair of mill-wheels."

They settled down together over the pile of peas, Betty fitting comfortably enough into her old place, yet aware of herself as an outsider now, startled and diverted by the constant comings and goings in the large room she had so recently taken for granted; the little boys on the hearth; men climbing down into and up from the cellar, checking on bottles and casks; the dairymaid bringing in milk and butter; a groom standing in the doorway – "them muddy boots does not touch my sanded floor" – while he munched his way through a hunk of bread and cheese; a scared-looking little maid asking "Please, Mum, her other ladyship's lady's maid is calling for a fresh posset for her, she says as the last one is tainted".

She exclaimed over the marmoset, kneeling down beside the fire with the boys to stroke it, but he became shy and hid his head in the shirt of his friend. Sarah explained how the mistress had taken a fancy to it when she went away to Harrowgate, "and a right worrit it be, Betty, for nothing you put down will be where you left it, for the little varmit has gone and took it for all its winning ways." The pages grinned and nodded, teeth and eyes brilliant in the firelight.

"But Betty, we heard as how you'd been took away for good, and your John swore a terrible oath as you'd never again set foot in this place. And now you say John will call here to pick you up when it is time to go home. Isn't it true then, and are you to come back after all?"

"Did you not hear about the riot and the burning of the house at the turnpike? 'Twas my mother's sister was burnt out of house and home and she had her little boy the next day. He is to be called Peter. They are all staying at my other uncle's, and my mother has been with her to look after them all (for her husband was sorely hurt). I came over today to bring my niece Nell back to her mother, and to fetch some baby clothes from the chest. And Mother says Aunt and the baby are much better now, and so is Uncle, so we all talked together and they told me all about that terrible night and especially how two of the servants of the hall found them by chance and helped them to safety, for they would all have perished without their help, and I asked Mother if I could try and find them and thank them, and she said I might, so long as I was ready to come back when John came for me. So here I am."

Betty had not noticed Celestine, who had caught the girl's words and was now listening keenly to the conversation.

"Nay, I know nothing of that, Betty. If 'twas any of us, she's keeping mum about it, perhaps she was where she no business to be, for all I know. But I am so glad to see you. You know I was right all the time. I told you that…. Thing…. I saw would bring bad luck, and then that poor man was killed, foully done to death in the night."

Mrs. Sanderson cut in. "Waste no tears on the likes of him. A worser man I never knew. He was one to make all he could out of other folk's misfortunes. 'Twas a bad day for many when his Lordship took a fancy to hire him for a druid."

Sarah asked, "How did that come about, then? I never thought of where he come from, it seemed he had always been here."

"He had been there all your life and more. A good fourteen or fifteen years back it must be. His Lordship took a sudden fancy, the way great folks will from time to time, and must needs have his ring of stones, and a cave, and a druid – that's a kind of wild man – to live in them. Proper heathenish, I call it."

"But what a strange occupation!" cried Betty. "Whatever can have made him willing to take on such strange duties – never being like himself, always in outlandish clothes, pretending to be-"

"Ah well, they do say that come natural-like to him on account of his being one of them wandering players as had fallen on hard times. And they say he heard Lord

Fenborough was wanting himself a druid and he waylaid him by the roadside. Old Charley was the groom riding with him and he says the fellow leaped into the road with tangled hair and a great grey beard right in front of his Lordship's horse, and held it by the bridle and talked to him. He could not hear what passed, but he said Lord Fenborough seemed in high good humour after he had gone and said, 'My own druid will be here tomorrow in his cave. And I warrant that I will keep him longer than my brother did his hermit!' And that he did, for he came the very next day and stayed fifteen years until his throat was cut!"

"And is it quite sure, " asked Betty quietly, "that he had been a player?"

"Nothing about him was sure, my duck. It is certain that no-one has ever claimed to be kin to him, or to have known him as a child. And you could never credit a word he said – not that he said a deal about himself at all – but 'twas thought in the kitchen 'twould fit well with his deceiving ways and clever pretences. And I do know he could read, though he made no show of it, and once, when he came into the kitchen soon after he arrived he talked about playing in a town and taking the part of a great man."

"You are not listening, Betty," complained Sarah, tugging at her friend's arm as she stared into the fire with a frown. "They say it was a gypsy who cursed him for he crossed her, and I did hear that they went out after her two nights back and near caught her – but she changed her shape to a hare by her magic arts an d got away, and all that were pursuing her suffered the next day with cramps, and sickness, and terrible headaches."

"Hold your tongue girl. Such foolishness has no place in my busy kitchen. Gypsies and witches indeed! If you must talk, talk of better things."

"Well, we have excitement enough here, too, everyone has come here for tonight, almost all her Ladyship's family. You'll recall when her Ladyship's mother last came at Easter time. I dussn't look at her, nor even at Miss Millicent."

Betty laughed gently. "You're a foolish one, Sarah. Miss Mighty Millicent is but a servant for all her airs and graces. My father's sister who farms her family lands and weaves her own cloth and sells at her own price is better than she is, for she has neither master nor mistress. 'Tis not the silk makes a lady. You do not need to tell me that the house is full. I can see that fine by the bustle in the kitchen. But tell me, Sarah," lowering her voice, "how goes it with you, yourself. Are you still being troubled by fancies of evil? Come now, I can see that you are. Tell me what you are afraid of."

"'Tis all foolishness, I suppose, but Betty, I did see – last night – I did see the Monk again in the passage and this time he turned his head and looked right at me. I know he did, for all I put my hands across my face."

"You saw what he looked like, then?"

"No, no I did not, you see, he had his hood down low, and then when I saw him, I screamed out loud. I could not help myself. Then he began to turn that great hood and I thought – I thought, what if there is no face inside that hood, and I closed my eyes so as not to see …. and where will it all end? I'm so afraid Betty."

"Do you wish to come away with me when John comes for me? We'll say you have been taken ill."

"What, and lose my post here? And the little presents I will get tonight when I am serving them all? And the pretty compliments when the wine flows free? And the left over junkets and ices? And not see all the great ladies in their fine clothes and the handsome young men? No, no, I will stay. I will do my best to forget my foolishness and carry on with my work."

Then Sarah was summoned to the kitchen garden, while a glance from the cook kept Betty busy with the peas. Celestine saw that the girl's face was troubled in the firelight. The finished gown was now lying across a clean table, covered with a white cloth, so she took the seat Sarah had left and began to help Betty with the peas. After a few moments Betty turned towards her and shyly addressed her:

"Oh, Miss. I was wondering if it was you that was so good to my mother's sister when their cottage was burnt down?" Celestine nodded and Betty went on, "I know now as there was nothing bad that night when I helped you with your young lady. It did trouble me in my mind, with it being when that man was killed, but the Good Book told me I should keep quiet and I am so glad I did. I would not make trouble for you and your lady for ever so much now. But can I have some private talk with you Miss? I am very put about by some news I have just heard and I do not know what I should think."

Celestine picked up the gown. Come upstairs with me. My mistress has gone out riding, and we can sit in my little room next to hers and be free from all interference."

And there, upon the window seat, while Celestine made one more lace ruffle for the neck of Araminta's gown and Betty straightened the skeins of silk in the workbox, she told her grandmother's story. "I don't know as she might be confused in her mind, for all I have never heard her so before, and I don't see there's nothing to be done, but I was all shook up when Mrs Sanderson said that about the druid, but I won't say nothing to nobody else, and I won't go getting tangled with great folks and the law, not no how."

Soon she slipped away to find to find her friend, but Celestine sat making lace, her mind weaving conjectures as intricate as the threads beneath her nimble fingers.

Friday evening

Dearest Louisa

It is now dark, and soon Celestine will be coming in to dress my head and array me for tonight's diversion. All day there has been a great bustle of preparation throughout the house. I looked into the great ballroom this morning and watched a small army of footmen on stepladders polishing the crystal drops on the two giant chandeliers, and fitting hundreds of candles into them and the sconces all round the walls. It will be as bright as day! And all the thousands and thousands of shadows will dance on the walls, and everybody's faces, and all will be strange and beautiful. Lovely little gilt chairs and tables were being put into position around the walls. The connecting room was lined down two sides with long tables, covered with stiff linen cloths so white I shall be terrified of taking anything from a dish for fear of leaving a stain on their virgin snowfields! Maids were carrying in baskets of silver and crockery. You would like to see the china: it is all painted in reds and blues with exotic birds and animals, and all has a gold rim and details of the painting also picked out in gold. All manner of enticing odours have been floating upwards from the kitchen; in short, all has been in a state of the most delightful excitement.

I cannot well understand Lady Fenborough. She has been all day with her maid, while I, if I were ever to be mistress of such a house, and the hostess to such a ball – not that I would ever wish to be mistress of this house – would not be able to keep myself away from supervising the preparations, and, I suppose, getting in the way of all the staff. Perhaps it is as well I shall never be a great lady!

This morning Letty and I went riding with Edward, Henry and Elizabeth. John and James took out guns with Frederick and William. I greatly enjoyed myself. Elizabeth may be a beauty, but she is no horsewoman. Poor Brownie fidgeted and shuffled, never sure what he was required to do by his rider who held the reins most awkwardly and was more troubled for her hat's wellbeing than her horse's. Letty, though sometimes nervous, rides well, and so do the two young men, especially Henry, who was on hand to calm Brownie when he shied, startled by a combination of a loudly barking terrier and an almost as loudly shrieking rider.

After a while he and I found ourselves ahead of the rest, by no design I assure you. We talked about our homes, and I told how, within our father's lifetime, England's last wolf had been killed on Humfrey Head, not twenty miles from where we live. He argued we could not be sure it was the last, and I said we could, for no more lambs had been lost, and it is not in the nature of wolves to live unnoticed.

His home is no great distance from Letty's and so he knows this countryside well. He said he knew of no wolves in the area, and believed there had been none for long enough, the wild country people were wolves in their hearts, for all their human shape. I thought of the poor murdered druid, and he said he was sure it was some rustic quarrel that had caused the dreadful crime. He told me the people were little better than ruffians and bandits, most of them, and when I recalled the burnt-out turnpike cottage

I had no wish to gainsay him. He says there have been riots again and again – when lands are enclosed sometimes a gang will come at night – women as well as men – and throw down the lawfully placed fences. "They do not even respect religion," he said. "Not long ago they all but killed a poor harmless man who fancied he was called upon to preach to these people in the open air and reform them – he should have saved his breath and his ribs, poor fool."

Then he told me about another strange thing. He asked me if I had ever heard of a "hedge priest". I told him no, and asked him to explain.

"'Tis a priest, or a man who was one formerly, with no benefice or pulpit; perhaps he has been expelled, or has taken himself to the countryside for his own disreputable reasons, and he makes his living by conducting clandestine marriages." Only think Louisa! I had always thought clandestine marriages came only in stories, and the over the border at Gretna Green, yet in this very countryside where I am staying is one who not only conducts them but is said to make his living by it! I will certainly ask Letty more about this. I think she might have told me herself, for we both love the romantic and picturesque, perhaps more so in books than in real life.

I do not think I would really wish for a secret marriage in a disused barn by night, with a lookout in case Papa had caught wind of it and was coming to disrupt our ceremonies…. Though it might have its attractions were the bridegroom of sufficient excellence!

Then Henry and I had a fine gallop before we returned to the others. Elizabeth was bareheaded and rather dishevelled;

Brownie had taken her under a tree where a low-hanging branch had caught in the feathers of her hat. We passed the tree on the way back, and there was the splendid hat, caught in the tree like some bird of paradise, spinning and swaying in the stiff breeze. I could not help smiling, and I thought of Absalom in the Bible, who was so proud of his hair and got it caught in a tree. Later I went down to the stables and gave Brownie an especially good apple.

I suppose it is to be expected that Letty will wish to spend her time with her cousins, and I am sure they do not wish to make me uncomfortable, but I do feel strange with so many new people, who have all known each other all their lives. I am so glad Letty told me that Margaret and Lydia Fairlight , who were at school with us, will be here tonight, and some of our other school friends whose names you will not know.

By the way, Henry also asked me for the first two dances. What bliss to tell him I was engaged! When I heard him asking Elizabeth two hours later, and her accepting, I felt so pleased. I also began to feel a little ashamed of my delight in her discomfiture on the ride.

Oh Louisa, I wish you were with me, and we could go down together!

Celestine has just come in and told me it is time to prepare. I think I shall not present a contemptible appearance. I am so looking forward to this ball. I shall write and tell you every detail tomorrow.

Your loving

Araminta.

The next day Araminta wrote again.

Saturday October 23rd

Oh dear, dearest Louisa,

It is all so horrible. How I wish I was at home! I will never never be able to forget it – every time I close my eyes it is all there in front of me again. What an ending!

But I will try to tell you about it calmly so that you can understand. Celestine says it will be better to write it all down for you. I do hope father will be able to come for us soon.

At first all was well. I saw in my glass that I was in good looks as Celestine placed the late roses she had gathered in my hair and at my bosom. And the red silk swirled around me beautifully. I was so pleased - and she had made it for me so quickly with all that lovely lace – I threw my arms round her and kissed her. Then I took up my fan and made my way downstairs. I was glad that I met Letty at the door and could go in with her. I felt suddenly very awkward. But I need not have feared. Nobody seemed to notice our entrance but we were soon part of a chattering crowd and I had no need to suppose that I would have to content myself with watching others dancing. All that early part of the evening now seems such a long time ago – dancing in line, spinning down the set, laughing, talking, flirting, sitting on one of the little gold chairs with my next partner while the last one brought me a glass of wine. Once I caught Lady Hastings' eye, while I was talking with Henry, and I do not think she looked best pleased with me.

Perhaps I was over excited, for I let her see I had noticed her scrutiny by smiling and waving and her face became frozen and she turned away. Once Letty and I walked out with our partners – the twins – on the broad walk outside the main windows, enjoying the contrast of the merriment behind us and the peace of the lawns and woods at which we gazed. I thought I discerned the movement of deer in the distance, while the music reached out through the yellow window spaces and lured us back into the dance and the blaze of trembling candles.

I wished the night to last for ever. How delightful it is when we realise that more than one pair of eyes is following our every movement, while we are in thrall to none, glancing around at will for pure enjoyment. The only slight shadow was that Letty seemed troubled; she had already danced with William and was covertly watching him, and I must own that his demeanour was not that of a young man about to propose marriage. I tried to comfort her, and told her he was not so very handsome (which is true, although he is much pleasanter than many a more dashing beau) and that she had been unsure whether she could ever care for him but she looked down, twisting her handkerchief between her fingers and muttered, "I am so afraid he will be angry – but I have done nothing, I cannot make him speak, and now he seems not to see me at all."

My indignation towards her brother grew, and I was not in the most agreeable of humours towards him when it was time for him to lead me to the set. He too seemed not much minded for conversation, so we began in silence. Just as I was trying to think of a suitable question to ask him about his day's sport (for I could not ask him the real question that exercised my mind – "Why are you so eager for your sister to accept William if he asks for her?") – Oh dear, it was so horrible – the noise and the darkness and the screaming!

I happened to be looking towards the great windows which overlooked the grounds – they were unshuttered for the sake of the moonlight – when suddenly a figure appeared at one of them. He must have been on horseback, although only the upper part of his body was visible. It might have been any young man with a dark cape over his coat but for the face. It was covered by a black mask with holes for the eyes. For a split second he looked at the scene. It seems to me now that I caught the cold glint of his eyes, but that might be the witness of terror, not eyesight. He smashed the window glass with a shocking crash. Then, with deliberation, he raised his pistol and fired twice into the hall. Immediately the two great chandeliers spun round and crashed to the floor – as they fell little pieces of rainbow coloured light danced wildly around the walls and ceiling, there was a terrible crashing sound and glass flying through the air – I was cut on the cheek and neck - and the hall was plunged into darkness as the thousands of candles fell to the floor or were blown out by the sudden wind which streamed in through the jagged edges of glass. The rider was now black against a blue-grey sky. He made no move to enter or speak, and all seemed frozen in terror. Then Frederick muttered something, broke away from me and charged towards the window. We could all hear the shards of glass tinkling and shattering under his boots, as he strode after the strange horseman. Then, unbelievably, the intruder turned his horse and made off into the night. We heard Frederick call for his own horse as he leapt through the window, then a second pounding of hooves followed the first into the distance.

In the ballroom now all was noise and sickening confusion. Ladies were screaming and I felt very alone standing by myself in the darkness afraid to move on the glass-strewn floor in my light slippers and with no protector. Most of the dancers had thrust their ladies behind them when the figure first appeared. I was afraid I would be thrown to the ground and trampled in the press and there was nobody to turn to for help. Then I felt a touch on my shoulder and heard the voice of William: " Let me carry you to the supper room. There will be some light there, and I will fetch your maid to you." I was never so delighted to hear a voice in my life, and as he picked me up I felt as though I could not have stood for another second. By this time everyone was searching for the doors and we were much jostled by the throng, so that William had much ado to keep his footing. How terrible would have been the injuries of anyone forced to the ground and stamped into the glassy fragments!

We made towards the edge of the room and above the screaming and wailing I heard Lady Hastings' cold voice. "Really Edward! If Elizabeth must swoon at such a time, leave her to her attendants. It is your duty to impose some order on this rout. Here, you!" – I suppose she clutched a passing arm –"go and tell the household servants to bring all the spare candles they can muster here, and take hot water and bandages to the supper room." Lord Fenborough clearly was loath to leave his wife but called out in a calm manner, "If you can do so, will you make your way to the supper room. Lights will be brought as soon as possible so that we can see what has been done."

Then I was sitting, leaning over one of the long tables, the blood from my neck dropping on the clean linen, and I looked up to see William shouldering his way through the press towards me, pulling Celestine behind him Just as she was applying a cloth to staunch the blood – and remember Louisa, all around us were the injured, some terribly hurt, some in a swoon, others jerking and shrieking in hysteria – there was an odd little silence and Frederick reappeared at the door on to the balcony. He was pale and his right hand was clenched tightly round his left arm just below the shoulder. I saw a dark stain spread beneath his fingers on the pale grey sleeve – and knew no more until I found myself in bed, with Celestine bringing me a comforting drink which sent me to sleep – a sleep in which I saw the man at the window again and again, and each time he was larger and more horrible in appearance until he changed into the monk and when he turned his head to me I saw he had no face but a skull, and I cried out and came to myself to find Celestine sitting beside me holding my hand. I do not know how many times this happened, but the last time it was broad daylight.

Celestine tells me that Frederick is not, so it seems, seriously wounded. He must have been hit by the villain as he pursued him through the night, but she says it is only a flesh wound. I do hope so. I cannot help thinking of my dream of the gypsy and what she said to Letty, for there is no doubt that Frederick is the dearest person in her life. I have not much liked him, but I must own he was braver than anyone else to rush upon the intruder as he did. I have not seen Letty or anyone else yet today.

But you must see that I wish to come home, for I feel I will never be comfortable again. And there are other things too, which I cannot set down on paper but long to tell you all about face to face. It is by the grace of God that neither of us has been killed.

All my love from your distracted

Araminta

* * *

With this letter went another ...

Dear Madam,

I do hope the master can come soon to take dear Minta home. She is almost out of her mind with fears and perturbations and I believe she indeed may be in some danger. The cuts she mentioned are not deep, and should leave no scars. I do not think she and I should travel unprotected for a reason I will tell you but dare not write. I have told her her father could not be here before Wednesday at the earliest, but please urge to come as soon as he can.

It is such a pity that a visit so eagerly anticipated should end like this.

Your obedient but sorely troubled

Celestine.

Celestine sealed both letters and set them aside for Porrott to take to the mail coach, then set herself to keeping watch over her young mistress. She did not intend her to discover that Sarah's body had been found that morning. Her head had been forced down into the waterbutt and held there until she drowned.

Araminta and Celestine sat huddled over the dying fire; dying because who could tell if the bell in the room would be answered. It seemed unlikely amid all the disturbance that a dutiful footman would appear with a full coal scuttle. They shivered in the chilly room, frightened and not knowing what to do for the best

Araminta glanced at her stained, once beautiful gown and shuddered at its brightness. There had been so much blood last night. Her face and neck stung with the cream Celestine had applied. She could not control her tears. Poor Frederick. How fearless he had been striding through the shards of glass. Had the masked rider been caught? Where had he come from? Where was Letty? How many of the guests had been killed or hurt? She wept for them all, for Frederick and Letty, for her fellow guests. Some of her tears were for the ravished ball, some for the lost gown.

Hooves were heard at the front of the house. It was now nine o'clock and the surgeon was riding away. Celestine beckoned Araminta and they stood at the window, watching, trying to read his impassive face.

His departure was noted from many rooms. Speculation was rife. Had he gone to summon assistance? How long had he been there – no one had seen him arrive. Whom had he been treating? " How serious he looks. I wonder how many patients needed his attendance?" " Why is the house so quiet? " "How many have been killed? Did his young lordship manage to strike down the intruder? Was he alone or with accomplices?" "Who were they and what was their purpose?" Endless variety of question but in the end, every heart swung like the compass needle to the long cry, "When can we go home?"

More hooves. Two more horsemen at the front entrance. As the grooms came out two gentlemen of middle age climbed down, and so we recognised them as magistrates. Lord Fenborough met them at the door and hurried inside with them.

Within a few minutes, a footman came to each guest room inviting them all to gather in the morning room, where breakfast had been set out.

They gathered there, subdued. No point in shrieking hysterically now; no one had a monopoly of horror. Why risk a sore throat when no one might notice. They listened dull as Lord Fenbrough apologised to them all for the distress caused by last night's intrusion. He told them that his son was not seriously injured; that beaters had been out searching the grounds from first light but had seen no one. Those who had been intending to go home might do so; one of these magistrates would visit them during the next few days in an attempt to cast light on the unfortunate event. . Here he introduced Sir Gregory Dawson and Mr Ambrose Monkhouse.

Someone asked, "Was anyone hurt besides your

courageous son?" "None known to you. I am sorry to say that one of the kitchen maids has been found lifeless in a water butt this morning. It is not yet known how she met her death." He was interrupted by cries of alarm and distress. " The local constable is investigating. This does not necessarily involve the intruder we all saw."

Lord Fenborough would be most grateful if the departing guests would maintain discretion about the recent distressing events. He had no wish for investigations to be hampered by vulgar curiosity. He gave his wife's apology for not coming to bid them farewell, but she wished to spend the day tending Frederick.

They ate quietly, saying little but eagerly preparing the stories with which they would regale their own neighbourhoods, once away from Skells and their hosts admonitions.

As soon as could be arranged they took their departure, Lord Fenborough and Lady Hastings bidding them farewell. All had gone by teatime.

Saturday

I find I must keep the more diligently to my journal, both to have clear in my own mind the troubling events that press upon us, and because I feel I may at some time have to acquaint my mistress with something of what has passed. There should be no need for a third reason.

I watched over Araminta after I had brought her from the ballroom until she slept, and remained by her in my chair, dozing but lightly. I was afraid; fearful lest her injuries and distress following so close upon great excitement would for a while send her entirely distracted, and even more fearful lest the one who had left his work uncompleted should return in the night to silence any who might be able to betray his identity. For who can doubt that the monk and the strange rider are one and the same? Yet why did he not strike harder when he could? But I do not doubt it was he who so cruelly murdered poor Sarah, a child so foolish she would blab whatever she might guess to the whole household.

Later in the morning there was a tap on the door and Letty entered. The poor girl had for once taken no thought for her appearance; her hair was roughly tied back, she wore her fine dress carelessly and her eyelids were red and puffy. She ran across the room and flung her arms around Araminta, begging her to stay and comfort her. Then she ran out to try to gain admission to her brother's room, or to hear news of him, while I hastily dressed my charge and dispatched the letters. I did not intend to give my soft-hearted young lady the opportunity to change her mind about going home to safety. When Letty returned, far sooner than I would have thought possible, the two girls sat by the window, Letty wailing and crying over her brother and Araminta, like the good-hearted girl she is, trying to comfort her.

"They will not let me see him and I am sure he is going to die! Perhaps he has been killed already and they dare not tell me. Mama is with him, and Papa is seeing to our guests as they depart with Grandmama's help, and I have nowhere to come but here. Oh Minta, Minta, I cannot bear it if my brother is to die."

"It is of no use to say you cannot bear it, Letty, for if it comes you will have to, whether you can or no." Araminta was much moved, and I know she was thinking of her own little brother's death, which she took very hard. "But," she continued more cheerfully, "I do not suppose it will come to that. I saw him, you know, when he came back. He was hurt in his left arm, but a broken arm will not destroy a young man. Last year one of my cousins took a fall out hunting and broke his arm, but he was abroad again, with his arm in a sling, in a few days. Come now, Letty, surely you know how irritated young men can become if their mothers and sisters show overmuch concern for injuries they themselves make light of. If you were crying like that it is no wonder they would not let you in to see him."

I must have fallen asleep, for when I next looked at the fire it had almost burnt out. The girls were sitting close together in silence. There was a sharp rap at the door and Leonie came in.

"My mistress would like to see the young ladies in the drawing room."

"Oh – has she left him then? How is he? Does this mean he is much worse and she has sad news to break to me?"

Leonie looked at first disinclined to make her an answer, but Letty's unhappiness must have moved her, for she replied in a less cold voice than is customary with her, that his young lordship was doing very well, for it was but a flesh wound with no bones broken, only the surgeon had bidden him keep his room for the day. It was almost distressing to see the sudden change in the child's face; her eyes glowed and little red patches appeared in her cheeks. She breathed deeply, cried, "Come on Minta, we must not keep Mama waiting", seized her friend's hand and dragged her from the room..

After a while it seemed to me that I should seek out Porrott and tell him what I knew of Sarah and the monk. I cannot forget that shrouded figure. Even as Leonie followed the young ladies out of the room, I thought that even she, in patterns, could have been the phantom. 'Tis an excellent disguise, for the long robe conceals the figure as completely as the hood hides the face, and I could not guess whether it was male or female, stooping to conceal height or upon patterns to increase it. But I suspect Porrott is intending to seek it out and I do not care for the way it has no mercy on those it catches unawares.

When I reached the kitchen it was awash with tears. The servants were busy enough, sweeping up debris and sorting out the mess of broken crockery, glass and food in the ballroom and the supper room with set faces. The cook was sitting by the kitchen fire with a weeping woman I did not know, but supposed to be poor Sarah's mother, for she kept saying "She was a good girl was my Sarah. She would never have destroyed herself or gone a wicked way. Who would kill her? She was a good girl, she was." Alas that folly and a loose tongue should be so dreadfully requited. They told me that the constable's men, having created great disturbance among the grieving servants in kitchen and stables, had to search for signs of intruders in the kitchen garden.

I had no wish to be observed and was glad to take some sticks of sugar from the kitchen to give to the horse Araminta rides while she is here and its stable companion. Behind the stables is a harness room, with a few stools and a fire. This was where I hoped to find Porrott. I heard his voice as I approached and hesitated. I had to speak to him in private and had no mind to be taunted by ribald stable lads. But I had the sugar with me, and surely I could ask his protection when I went into the stables to feed the horses without arousing suspicion. I looked cautiously in through the doorway. Porrott was sitting on a bench, the two little pages beside him, and he seemed to be drawing something in a little book for them. I knew the book for one Araminta told me she had given to Jacko with a little tasselled pencil, and sure enough, there was Jacko perched on the window sill (the boys had changed his chain for a much longer fine rope.) It pointed and chattered at me and jumped down to the boys. All three looked up as I explained my errand. At the word "sugar" three pink palms were thrust under my nose and six dark eyes gazed meltingly into mine. I laughed and broke up some of the sugar for them. Porrott turned to the pages. "You had best go back to the kitchen. It is near the time my lady has her chocolate and you will be needed. Put the little beast back on his chain and be off with you."

For a minute they acted like the little boys they are, dodging around the room giggling, leaping from stool to chest to stool while Porrott tried in vain to catch them; then suddenly their faces became still and hidden again, they picked up the braided coats they had hung on the hook behind the door, put the chain on the monkey and trudged back to the house – but Jacko leapt around them, landing on the shoulder of first one then the other, for all the world like a good parent trying to show no partiality between her children.

"They come in here sometimes. There is nothing the monkey can damage so he can have more liberty. I was just showing them how to write his name. Then I will teach them to write theirs. It is not much, but it may help them a little on the hard road before them. I have no idea where they found the little book and I do not intend to ask."

I laughed. "You need not fear. It was a present from Araminta to Jacko in the coach going home from Harrowgate. She told me about it; she was much diverted. It seems the little brute snatched one of my lady's emerald earrings that she was carrying in her purse to get repaired at the jeweller's. Her Ladyship was much disconcerted by the theft, and Araminta got it back by offering him the little book and pencil. Then he jumped out of the coach where it was stopped by the burnt-out cottage and came back with a ruby pin which he presented to her. She says he was most annoyed when Lord Fenborough took it to give to the constable."

Now I had seen Porrot I was ashamed I had ever wondered if he might be the monk. And I liked him the more for his kindness to the little pages.

"Is it not a pity," I said, "that Jacko cannot write or speak. He goes everywhere, sees and hears everything. If only he could put it all down in the little book perhaps all the mystery would be resolved."

"I feel for the poor creature. It must be bored to distraction. I know how he feels, for people talk before us too as if we had no sense. I suppose to many of our betters we are nothing but rather bigger pet apes, without tails, but more useful, and kept on somewhat longer chains."

`"But if we are-"

"Then we should be able to discover what is happening far better than the law officers before whom all hold their tongues. Yes, how do you like the idea, you and me together – a pair of rational apes; watching, listening, remembering, thinking and finding a solution. But I have been waiting to see you. Are you sure you took no hurt last night?"

I explained I was not in the ballroom at the time of the shooting and went on to let him know that the young maid who was killed in the night had been telling all and sundry how she had seen the monk and he had turned to face her.

He grasped me by the wrists and leaned forward, "Celestine, you must take care. Tell no-one, man or woman, what you have seen. If you chance to see this monk again do not let him see you and escape as soon as you can. Do not be alone at night."

I told him I was not as brave as I had thought, and would indeed leave ghost hunting for the future. There was that in his gaze I have no time to consider at the moment; only I own the recall of it does not displease me.

"Now do you tell me," I countered, "have you yourself prudently avoided the sinister monk? I should not be best pleased to find you in the water-butt tomorrow, for I would then be unable to take any rain-water for my complexion."

"I know something. I thought I had found out his identity but I am confused now, and perhaps my ideas are all wrong. But there is something important to tell you. I went out yesterday morning to the place you indicated – nay there can be little risk in broad daylight – and tried the stone you told me of. And I found this."

He lifted the lid of a chest containing horse-cloths, delved down the side and produced an old wooden box. He handed it to me. I opened it and saw a number of letters, some of considerable age, a little note book and a number of pieces of jewellery.

"Why ever did you take these? They must be stolen, Oh, put them back before there is a search."

"You are right, indeed you are. The jewels will go back tonight, and the box, but not, I think the letters. Look at the inscriptions. What do you notice?"

I examined them - there were about half a dozen – and noticed they were all in different hands, to different people. One, to the rector of the parish, was in a foreign handwriting. The others were to various ladies of whom I had never heard.

Porrott looked seriously at me. "I think this is the Druid's 'treasure' that he had hidden away. I have looked at one of the letters and it is such that should never have been written to a married lady and, once written, should certainly never have fallen into any hands but hers. Look at the notebook.!"

It contained a number of entries in a villainous hand, all of the same form, an initial followed by various sums of money, all dated. Some of the entries went back almost fifteen years, others had been but recently begun. In two cases the name had been scored out, and the words 'felo de se' scrawled underneath. Then I realised what I held and flung the book to the floor. "I think the cook was right when she said the Druid was no loss! He must have been extorting money for his silence year after year – what pain he must have given them – and did you find the harvest he reaped with this twisted sickle?"

"I did not… I am glad of it, for 'twould be a sore trial of any man's honesty when the fellow left no heir that I know of… I think there can be no doubt our devout friend had a very profitable business. The question is, what do we do with these? He tapped the pile of letters. "We can put them back and forget we have seen them. Then the monk – or whoever has stolen them – can set himself up in succession to the Druid. We can try and return them to their owners, which could prove sad if either we were detected or they fell into the hands of their nearest but not dearest. Or we can burn them – but then the owners will not know that they are safe. The fourth possible course I won't sully your ears with. I promise you that all I found is here."

"Burn them, burn them now before my curiosity gets the better of me. My fingers are itching to discover – especially the rector – but no, put them all in the fire."

Together we tore them up and watched them burn. Had I been alone I could not but have read them first. It is better as it is. The flames died, the fragments turned red, then black, then grey. Porrott crushed them to powder with the poker, saying, "What a load of guilt and sorrow has gone up in smoke!"

I had been thinking of those from whom the letters had been stolen. Perhaps they had been receiving just retribution for past wickedness, but I thought of them suffering for years for a single indiscretion, wept for and repented countless times. How anxious their hearts must be at this time. Then I saw how they could be reached.

"Porrott, " I said, "my mistress once lost an engraved watch in the street. The next day it was handed to the housekeeper by a stranger. My mistress was out visiting at the time and he went away without leaving his name. As she wished to thank him, she sent me out next day to place an advertisement in the paper, expressing her gratitude to the unknown honest man. Could we not ourselves put in an advertisement, something like 'Found at Skells; a packet of letter destroyed unread.' Only those whose letters were here would understand, and they would perhaps then feel safe."

Porrott took some persuading before he agreed, as he put it, to spend his hard earned shillings on providing peace of mind for ladies and gentlemen who were no better than they ought to be, but when he saw I was in earnest, I prevailed.

Then I thought I might be missed and returned to our room. Porrott has promised faithfully that he will return the jewels tonight.

So, I suppose the monk knew about the Druid's 'treasure' and killed him in order to steal it and use it for himself – but wait, that we do not know. It is almost sure it was he who stole it, but he may have found him dead. For had not the writers of these letters we had destroyed, one and all, good reasons for turning on their tormentor? Though I can hardly imagine that ladies of surrounding estates, however indiscreet their personal lives may have been, invading Skells by night with murderous intent.

And what of the masked man? Was he the monk? And why should he act as he did, whether he were or no?

So many questions I cannot answer. And a few terrifying facts:

• *The monk was abroad the night the druid was killed.*
• *So were Araminta and I.*
• *I believe we were watched in the Temple of Piety.*
• *The monk was abroad again on Friday night.*
• *A girl who boasted of seeing him was drowned on Friday night.*

Is it any wonder I long for us to be back at home?

Sunday October 24th

Autumn sun was pouring the windows in the south aisle. Lord Fenborough's father had had the clear glass put in, getting rid of the old-fashioned stained glass with its deep colours and stylised saints. The rector of the time had turned an elegant conceit on how the current Age of Reason (embodied in his patron's generosity) had dispelled from the church the gloomy half-perception of the Age of Superstition and enabled the Eternal Truth to be open before the eyes of all. The new windows certainly made it possible for the bored choir boys to study each ruffle, embroidered lappet and facial plane of the party from the house.

Unfortunately, thought Porrott, those behind were offered an equally splendid but far less revealing view. Usually when he drove the family to church he remained outside with the horses but today he had followed them into church where he now sat on the stone ledge by the door. He needed time to think and while the liturgy flowed past him as undemanding as the sunlight, his time was his own.

He was troubled, and to some extent vexed. His eye rested first on Frederick as he sat upright at the end of the pew. There was no denying his handsome appearance and stalwart mein. Only a slight rigidity of the shoulders as he took his seat betrayed any awareness of the keen interest his appearance had aroused - a man supposed to be at death's door after taking on four armed ruffians in single combat and losing, according to various sources, his right arm, the use of his legs, and most of the blood from his body. No wonder a whisper and rustle of astonishment had followed him up the aisle. Porrott frowned. He had been so sure of Frederick as his villain. He had had opportunity to judge his capacity for wickedness, and in this respect had not found him wanting. He could so easily have been the monk, with his ability to move unchallenged around the house and grounds at all times. If there was anything in the story that the girl who used to be one of the maids had told Celestine he, if anyone, had a good motive to silence the druid. He could have shoved a servant girl's head in the water butt with ease. Porrott craned his neck to examine the wrists where the lace ruffles fell away. No use, he was gloved. No chance of tell tale scratches there. It all fitted so well, but for the stranger at the ball. He, at least, could not have been Frederick; Celestine was adamant that her mistress had been with him, indeed, held in the dance by him, at the very moment the intruder appeared. And a hundred witnesses had seen him follow the man, had heard him ride off in pursuit of him. And he was sure that two strong arms would have been needed to drown poor Sarah when she came down to draw water for the kitchen. No, whatever evil was afoot, and however Frederick might be involved, he was not the source of it all.

Mr Charlton was sitting beside his friend, with a less confident carriage. He too should be thought on. None of the recent startling events had preceded his arrival. He could be the monk almost as easily as Frederick. Could not the druid have held some dangerous knowledge of him too? He was healthy and agile. Nothing of his character was apparent for good or ill. True, he was occupied with young Araminta shortly after the shots were fired; but might it not have been possible to ride away a short distance, strip off his disguise and return rapidly to the ballroom to rescue the young lady, thereby ensuring he had someone to vouch for him. One must not forget the darkness and confusion, the difficulty of judging intervals in such shocking circumstances. He seemed rather taken with young Araminta at the moment – he had just turned his head a little to look at her – but that did not automatically absolve him in Porrott's eyes. It might well disarm the partial Celestine though. But- and now his glance moved back to the next pew and rested on her demure hat and the dark hair showing beneath it.

She was worth the lot of them put together, with her clear way of thinking and her gentle courage. At first his interest in the crime had stemmed from curiosity and a tidy mind; now, because of her, he wanted the evil stopped, before it hurt her more. She must be kept safe. Wednesday was the day they were expected to leave. She put up her hand to adjust her mantle. He decided to waste no more of this peaceful time on the killings, and turned all his mind to watching her.

Celestine was well aware Porrott's eye was upon her. She had, ever since the ball, been counting the hours until she and Araminta might be safely away: only three more days – and yet, these days might leave her with much unfinished private business. A young woman of no family grows early accustomed to reticence and caution had become second nature. And so, why this certainty? He must surely say something before Wednesday. And how would Araminta react to her desertion? In time, and time she would give her, the girl's kindheartedness would triumph over any sense of loss or grievance. She might even revel in the romantic circumstances that had thrown them together, once it was all over. If only he could resolve these mysteries and dispel all danger from them. She had never been so sure of Frederick's guilt as he had seemed to be, and William was not a likely villain. How could he be when he had so kindly taken care of Araminta after the disaster? What then of his Lordship? He might well have a great reason for silencing his former servant, but the flamboyant circumstances of the druid's death, almost like a stage set up for a drama, surely could not be his. He would have no need of such meaures; it would be the action of a stupid man when he had so many opportunities to hand to arrange an unobtrusive accident, and stupid Lord Fenborough was not. Could one of the druid's victims have hired an assassin who have evaded detection in the grounds? Or even – she looked at the man in the pulpit, remembering the letter and the line of yews between churchyard and rectory. If only she could see his wrists and forearms clearly. She smiled at the absurdity of her picture – the handsome, lined face, the fresh –laundered vestments, the noble and authoritative voice; the owner of these drown a girl like a kitten? She saw again the seven year old Araminta, screaming and kicking the stable lad she had just found drowning a litter, and turned slightly towards her, noticing how her fingers were entwined tightly in her lap.

Araminta was on the verge of panic. How could they all sit so quietly in the sunlight, listening to the same words she heard every week, dressed in their best clothes. Someone, maybe one of the people in this church with her, maybe even someone she had met, was waiting to destroy her. How brave Frederick had been! She was sorry she had thought harshly of him, for he was the only one with the courage to hit out at the wickedness that was engulfing them. Another three days before she could look to see her father, "Please God let nothing happen before then, and please keep Letty safe after I've gone." Perhaps Letty could come back with them for a while. Surely any father would wish to have his daughter out of danger, and however little she understood Lord Fenborough, she was sure he loved his daughter.

Letty had been praying over and over, not daring to stop, "Thank you he's alive, please don't let him be angry with me, please keep him safe." He had teased her that morning when he saw her red eyes: "Cheer up, Mouse, I am not so easy to get rid of as all that. I'll warrant the fellow who put the ball into me is in far worse case himself." He had not yet asked her about William. Was her mother right in expecting William to speak for her? And if so, why had he failed to do so? Would her mother be angry too?

Lady Fenborough turned her head to keep the sun out of her eyes. She was bewildered and exhausted. The dark figure outside the ballroom window was constantly before her eyes. In the small hours he assumed an unearthly character. Why had he come? Was it Frederick he wished to destroy or the whole family? And Frederick hurt – not desperately, but so as to distress and torment her further. Then the deaths; it was the servant girl's that haunted her more. She had seen the girl in the yard on Friday, an entirely ordinary girl about her daily business. What a sudden visitor death could be! She could see nothing ahead, but more confusion and misery. If only her mother would go away. She could not bear any longer her ceaseless reminders of how she should conduct herself – and in her own house, too.

Lady Hastings was angry. She sat upright, wearing an expression of calm devotion, and only her maid could have guessed at the blazing rage within her. All her careful work for Elizabeth and the others ruined. Even if both deaths and the masked stranger were the work of a madman with no link with the house or family, the family must suffer. Great, even good ,families would be reluctant to form alliances, positions of honour would be forthcoming in neither church nor state. Did ever a woman have such ill fortune? That for which she had worked with neither respite nor relaxation since the age of twelve destroyed in a few days through no fault of her own. Of course, if Elizabeth had had more character she might have lessened the damage, but it was now too late. Perhaps she had better set some distance between this place and herself, to salvage what she could. Frederick's courageous action was the one redeeming feature. If only the ruffian could have been found dead with Frederick's ball in him. And how stupid of her son-in-law, with all the advantages of land-ownership and magistracy, not to have made sure that just such a body was found.

His Lordship was most uncomfortable. Not a reflective man, he had by instinct created for himself a home as he liked it in his own countryside. He was not sure of the best way to maintain this way of life. Above all, he was anxious about his dear Letty. But there was nothing he could do at the moment. Relieved for a time, of the responsibility of action, exhaustion overcame him and he took refuge from his troubles in unobtrusive sleep until roused after the sermon by his wife's nudge, much to the chagrin of the vicar.

William was thinking of a conversation he must have with Lord Fenborough. He might stay a few more days, perhaps long enough to keep an unobtrusive watch over young Araminta until her departure, but then he was going away. Several things were puzzling him greatly, besides the shocking public events. He needed to go away and think carefully about his future course of action. When he had seen his Lordship, he would make preparations for a swift departure if necessary. He would arrange with the groom – the one who had brought them to church – to have his horse saddled and ready at night.

And so they reasoned, sitting unhearing through the sermon, kneeling heedless of the blessing, and leaving the church careless of the people's vulgar curiosity.

Monday October 25th
The Octagon Tower

Monday afternoon

My dearest Louisa,

You would wonder at the place from which I am writing this letter. How I wish I could show it to you! It is a little eight- sided tower with windows on all sides and carved turrets on the corners of the roof, high up in the grounds of Skells among woodlands. I saw it from without when Letty first showed me the walks and the parkland, that day we encountered the sinister winding tunnel – which I would not go through now for a thousand pound, though it amused me then.

This morning, we were all uneasy and oppressed in spirit within the house. For myself, whether at table, in my chamber or in the drawing-room I could find no security; as we moved through the common offices of the day I felt as though I were dancing a quadrille on a quagmire. When we were in the music room I could not but reflect as I gazed up at the painted ceiling, on the wild beasts I felt sure were lurking in the thick woods surrounding the innocent nymphs and shepherds amid their fleecy delights. How helpless they all seemed, save the strong young hunter - and, in reality, he, too, is wounded..

Lady Fenborough keeps her room while Lady Hastings rules in the drawing - room, though Letty tells me her grandmother is unlikely to outstay us by many days. Poor Letty is still tearful, and starts at the slightest motion. We sat in the drawing-room after breakfast, with little conversation. I could see that Laura found us tedious company, yapping and making for the door whenever she could. The senseless beast could not understand the shadow which held us back from the bright sun. The morning was beautiful, and I longed for air and movement, but durst not propose a walk. Thinking of our walks in the grounds, I began to speak of this little tower, and Letty recalled it with pleasure to her father.

The upshot was, that Lord Fenborough proposed an excursion thither for us this afternoon. What a deal of preparation followed! Servants were dispatched to sweep it out, set a good fire in a brazier, and take up cushions and rugs for the furniture kept there. Then (though it is indeed no great distance to walk) a light carriage came for the three of us and is waiting, with two of the men, for when we wish to return. They are stationed beside the door. I saw they were armed, and will own I am glad of it. So now they stand without, to guard the path, while I look out of the window and write to you.

It is very quiet here. Letty fell asleep upon the sofa, for she has slept little these past few nights. Laura waited only for this to be let out and after the rabbits. She is not herself the size of a full-grown buck, but she is a plucky little beast. I leaned out of the window to watch her stout white body wriggling with determination through the trees and undergrowth beneath us. Any rabbit she catches must be blind, deaf and lame! When I turned to speak to Celestine

I saw she too was asleep. I have not woken her for I know she has been much tired with watching. I covered her with one of the wraps, and returned to my post to write to you.

It is a strange feeling when one's companions are asleep. I feel they are in my care in this beautiful and peaceful little room. The tower is at the top of a steep wooded slope and I see before me the varieties of greens, browns and golds as the trees begin to turn. The huge chestnut leaves are quite changed and will soon fall ; the others begin to follow. Down below are the lakes in front of the terrible Temple of Piety.

There are three of them – one like a circle in the midst with two curiously shaped on either side, the whole like a huge dead eye staring upwards. And my little eyes are gazing down, watching tiny figures moving along the paths; and my eyes too are in a measure blind, for one at least must travail under a burden of guilt and care, could my gaze but pierce into the heart. Then I thought there is One to whom all hearts are open and from whom no secrets are hid, and so the great unseeing eye upon the ground put me in mind of the greater all seeing eye in Heaven and I was in a small measure comforted.

Enough of such Sunday thoughts! We are perched here in our tower like three princesses in a fairy story; Sleeping Beauties my companions and myself, perhaps, Rapunzel. Though there is no young man I would risk my hair for here.

There are more people moving around than I thought there would be. Lord Fenborough and his steward have ridden along the main roadway towards the Abbey ruins, and a group of kitchen girls have come down with leavings for the ducks on the great lake to my right. Such a commotion they are making on the water – I see it all, but hear nothing. Two swans are gliding towards them, indolently as if they consider the mallard rabble unworthy of their attention, but keeping sharp eyes on the crusts in the water.

Then a phaeton comes briskly into view – their two ladyships. Lady Hastings is driving, very upright and decided in her bearing, as always. Perhaps it is because I am such a distance above them, and they do not see me, that I understand what I have never seen before, that Lady Fenborough is in deadly fear of her mother. What a strange thing for one of her years! I recall that many of my friends at school had not the blessing of a mother such as we have, and some were in stark fear of them (and some deserved to be, too.). Now I am older and have seen more of the world I suspect that the longing of some of them for husbands had a great deal more to do with the need to escape their mothers than romance, and I wonder if they found either love or escape. It is a shaming thing to see one grown woman afraid of another. I have made a vow dear sister, that never, never shall my daughters be afraid of me, even when I am an old lady of forty.

Something is afoot again over by the great lake. The girls have gone away, and as I thought the swans have pushed aside the ducks and moorhens, who have retreated to deeper water, grumbling and muttering like small boys driven from an orchard by the owner's unexpected return.

But now the swans take to the air – how clumsily they move off. Each time I see them attempt to rise from the water I expect them to fail. I like them the better for it. I think I would be rather in awe of their graceful perfection afloat and in flight were they not so awkward in changing from one to another. (Do you remember the day Lady Bakewell came to call on Mama; with what dignity she bore herself in coach and parlour, and yet she all but fell headlong down the steps of the coach? I remember we were all lined up beside the path to greet her, and I was sent back to the nursery in disgrace for smiling.)

Now I see why the swans flew off. One of the grooms – Porrott I think – is leading a young colt down to the water's edge for a drink. It is a pretty little chestnut that I have not seen before. The two little blackamoors are with him and – yes, there he is – the little scarlet dot is Jacko in his livery. But what is he about now? He has tied the colt beneath the tree and, looking over his shoulder in a furtive way, has slipped beneath the trees. Now he seems to be throwing something into the water. What terrible thing is this? Poor Celestine! But why bring the children with him if there is aught amiss. Again he throws, and again....ah, wait! I can see now what he is doing. He is skimming flat stones. The water is now so still that I can see from here the pattern of interlocking widening circles. All he is doing is teaching the little blackamoors to skim stones... well done! One of them has the knack already, .. three, four, five... now the other one, not so good. Jacko is throwing with them now, with vigour but no science. Porrott is very skilful... that one leapt a good dozen times... they have finished now, no more stones left. Do you remember how Tom taught us to skim stones on the little tarn at the top of our wood that summer? It seemed to me a marvel that a stone could jump on water. Indeed, it still does.

Speaking of Tom, that reminds me that Frederick's friend William knows him; indeed he says he owes his life to him. I discovered this only today. We were in the music room. I was accompanying Letty on the harp – which she plays far better than I – when she suddenly stopped, jangling the instrument, and fled from the room. As I rose to follow her, I saw William in the other doorway. He begged our pardon for startling us, and as I was gathering the music together added suddenly, " Miss Lewthwaite, have you a brother Thomas who is a captain in the 87th ? " You will guess I was all attention, and fearful lest this was bad news. He was pleased to say I had a look of him, though why he should think so when Tom is over six feet tall with luxuriant ginger whiskers I cannot imagine.

Then he told me about how he had met him once in an inn and how, enjoying the evening together, they determined to ride with one another the next day. Then he said that half a dozen ruffainly cut throats had rushed upon them with cudgels as they were resting under a tree at noon, "and," he said, "I do not believe I should be here to speak with you today but for your brother. He had his sword out in a trice and beat them off before I had managed to draw myself. 'Twas only yesterday I caught a look of him in you to be sure you must be his sister; even though, he told me his name was not so very unusual in his country."

Now is not that just what we would expect of Tom – such an adventure and he tells us not one word. How we shall tease him when we see him. But oh, how I wish he was here now with his good sword, then I should feel safe. You may well ask me where my love of adventure has gone – back between the pages of books, dear Louisa, where the story can always be put by. What I have to tell you now will explain why I feel this. I have shut it out of my letter with chatter about this and that, but cannot shut it out of my mind. And I feel I can no more keep silent than I could were you in reality by my side. Tell our parents if you think it good – but I hope Papa will be here by Wednesday night. I have tried not to increase your anxiety, but I am not strong enough.

After William had told his story and I exclaimed upon it he looked at me rather strangely and invited me to walk with him in the aviary "where we would not be caught unawares." Surely, I thought, he cannot mean to make an offer at such a time – and indeed I hoped not, for though I like him well enough I do not wish at all – not for a long time, and not so far from home. In my confusion I heard Celestine say that in the present danger she had no intention of allowing me to be alone, or with one other person, out of her sight. I was glad. William approved her caution, and the three of us moved into the long glazed building, where he sat with me on a bench beneath a palm.

"The birds will give warning of any approach," he explained

By now I had recovered enough self-possession to turn to

him with, "Well, sir?"

Now he seemed reluctant to begin. My eye fell on the top button of his coat and I watched him twist it this way and that as he gathered his thoughts and spoke. He asked why Letty had fled on his entrance, and barely listened to my excuses of her sudden faintness before asking if she thought she had any reason to fear him or if he had in any way displeased her. I could only shake my head, but he went on, "It is all since that terrible night. I danced with her early, and she seemed most anxious and ill at ease – almost, well, almost as if she was expecting something –"

I tried to deny this, but words failed me, and my hot face told him all he needed to know.

"But why?" he continued almost to himself. "I have given her no cause, and I could have sworn her own feelings were not…"

"But when her own brother tells her, sir, and he a close friend," I faltered.

He slapped his hand on his knee. "Aha! And can you tell me why that same brother should time and again assure me of his sister's great fortune (which she has not), excellent disposition and great love for me concealed only by her singular purity and modesty?"

"He has no right to speak like that," I rejoined hotly, "Nor you to listen!"

He sat gloomily twisting the button until he snapped the thread.

"Was that what you wished to say to me?"

"No, no, there is more, just give me a moment. I am no great talker and this is – but I must say – after all, Thomas's sister and all that – wouldn't like any sister of mine to be entrapped – least I can do for him."

Celestine rescued him. "You need not fear my mistress entertains any partiality for her friend's brother. His manner towards his sister is sufficient warning for any girl of sense."

He glanced at me to see I agreed, than let out a long sigh, stretched out his legs and thrust his hands deep in his pockets. After a while he spoke again, with much more coherence.

"It is not pretty to talk about one's host. But these are strange times. Have a care, ladies, I have to go away soon – do not trust Frederick, whatever you do, do not trust him."

I cried out in alarm but Celestine put her hand on my shoulder, and said quietly, "You have said too much to draw back now. You must not terrify us with vague hints. What do you know or suspect?"

Even then, he was not sure whether to speak. But at times spirit is stronger than station, and so it was that Celestine compelled him.

"I know him to be badly in debt from gaming, and that his father does not know this. I also know that he and some of his friends have at times recouped their losses by robbery upon the highway – though always hitherto without bloodshed."

"May I ask you, sir, why you are still his companion?"

He did not meet her eye. "Because I am weak. I told myself I was not sure, I did not want to be sure. He can be a fine, rousing companion, so I shut my eyes when I feared I might see something. But now ---"

"Yes?" she prompted. "What has changed your mind now?"

He looked around carefully, then leaned forward and spoke quietly. " Three things. First, what I have just learned. It seems to me he is trying to buy my silence and ensure that his disgrace would be mine by inveigling me into a marriage with his sister, who is a nice little girl and deserves far better than a husband who does not love her. Secondly, I went shooting with him the day after the fire at the turnpike and smelled smoke in his hair. And, most important, the night of the ball. I am not sure I did not recognise in the masked stranger one who is a mutual acquaintance, a wild young man fit to do anything for a wager. Moreover, when Frederick returned wounded he was mighty anxious to keep me away from his injured arm, but when he lost consciousness I was one who helped to undress and tend him. And the wound did not fit the story he told later."

"How ?"

"He said he had been shot from a fair distance, as the rider turned and shot from the saddle at his pursuer. But I have seen many bullet wounds, and this was fired from close at hand. I should say the gun was pressed against the flesh."

"But," I stammered, "does this not give us a second assassin?"

"No. I think what Mr Charlton believes is that for some reason Frederick inflicted the wound on himself. It is certainly in a less dangerous place than I would expect an assassin to choose at short range. Not even a broken bone, but a real enough injury. That is what you believe, is it not?"

"I fear it. And I dare not guess at why he should do it."

"But should you not lay this before- " I stopped

He laughed shortly. "Yes you see the problem. His Lordship is of course the magistrate in these parts. I am leaving soon. Then I will decide how I must act. Again, have a care,ladies."

He rose abruptly and walked out of the far door.

And so my dear, do you wonder I am afraid? I do not even know if his story is true, or made up to turn away suspicion from himself. I do not think he could be so wicked, but then, how could the other? I do know that until we leave this house Celestine and I lie together, behind locked doors with a candle burning. Pray God we come home safe. How I coaxed poor Mama to let me come here, and how sorry she would be…but no, we shall see you all within a week. I could wish you were with me but for the peril.
My dearest love to you all,
Araminta

PS. How strange that when I look up all is still so peaceful to the eye. As soon as I have sealed this I will call the servants and rouse my companions. The sun is sinking, and I would be within doors well before dusk.

Monday night

I write this in such fear and trembling that I can scarce hold my pen. All is quiet; Araminta is at last asleep, the fire is but red embers and the candle in the window burns away with a steady flame. It is near midnight but I cannot sleep. Indeed, I must not until I have set down what I have seen and heard – in case (which God forbid) mine should be the sole witness. Let me try to arrange my thoughts in the right order that my testimony might be clear.

I had determined to acquaint Porrott of what William had told us as soon as possible, and I had much ado, while dressing my young lady's hair for the evening to persuade her I must go out to the stables to do this. The best time would be while the family was at dinner and playing cards afterwards; I would not be missed and would be back – I promised her a dozen times – before it was time for her to retire. In the end she agreed. I was glad of it, for had she not I must have disobeyed. She was pale, but otherwise in good looks when she went down, with her head high and a dignity in her gait I had not noticed before.

I put on my cloak and slipped across the yard unobserved. For better concealment I took with me no lantern, When I reached the stables I found none there but the horses, but seeing the ladder to the hayloft I thought Porrott might well be taking his rest among the bales,. I went into the furthest recesses of the loft, it being difficult to see if anyone was there in the wavering shadows cast by the roof-beams, for the lantern was far away beside the door. At last I turned and looked down into the stables. I noticed a tankard and a hunk of bread on the bench beneath the lantern. The bread was wrapped in a handkerchief I knew to be Porrott's, so I made myself comfortable in the hay to await his return. I could see everything below without being seen by peering between two bales.

Soon footsteps approached. I was about to show myself, but drew back because they sounded wrong – too urgent for a groom about his regular business. Peering out, I saw Mr Charlton come in, dressed for travelling and carrying a dark lantern which he put out on entering the stable. He made his way to the stall directly beneath me, where I saw his own horse was tied, harnessed and ready for a journey. He bent to the horse's near front hoof, then to each in turn. The sound of its stirring in the straw altered; the hooves seemed somehow different. I realised that he must have muffled the hooves as Porrott had done the night of the fire. He must be eager to depart unheard, and no wonder, if he had spoken truly to Araminta. I wondered if he meant to tell his story elsewhere: I also wondered where he had learned the trick of muffled hooves, and what were his dealings with Frederick's association of wild young men. Then he untied his horse, led it out of the stall, and mounted. He gathered the reins – then checked.

In the doorway stood the Monk. I bit my hand to stop myself crying out and heard Mr Charlton draw in his breath sharply. The next moment the figure was beside the horse, and I saw a pistol in the right hand. The left arm moved stiffly to grasp the bridle, and as the horse reared the hood fell back. I saw it was Mr Frederick. He spoke to the rider, "So this is why you were not at dinner! What a way for a guest to depart. But you will have to wait: I need a mount now. Get down at once, with no sound."

I could not blame Mr Charlton for his trembling, with a pistol not a yard from his face. I saw his mouth working as he tried to speak.

Mr Frederick spoke again, "I have no time to waste. Get down now or I shoot." He swung himself down clumsily, one foot seemingly caught in the stirrup. As he reached the ground his foot slipped on the foul straw and he fell backwards, crashing his head against the solid manger. I could see blood pouring down his hair and neck, then soaking into the straw beneath him as he lay insensible, face down. Frederick was now in the saddle. The horse was restless at the commotion and smell of blood, and for a moment I feared it would lash out at Mr Charlton's prostrate body. Why does he not go now, I thought.

Then I saw the arm in its loose sleeve rise and level the pistol, as Porrott came through the door, whistling and carrying a kitten.

In a long moment Frederick fired, Porrott threw himself to the floor and I pushed with all my might at the hay bale in front of me. It fell to the ground just behind the horse and - as I hardly dared to hope – distracted Frederick long enough for Porrott to pick up a broom and dash the pistol from his hand. He swung again, this time at the body, but with a roar of pain and rage Frederick urged the big hunter straight at the doorway and was gone, the muffled hooves dying away swiftly.

In a moment both of us were bending over Mr Charlton..
He was still unconscious, but by the time I had washed the
blood away and bound up his head he began to recover. We
begged him to return to the house, but his one idea was to
get away to his friends. Seeing he would not be shaken, and
afraid lest fear and frustration should aggravate his injury
Porrott saddled him the quietest, most sensible mare in the
stables and let him go. He would not even suffer us to rouse
his manservant, but left the moment his mount was ready.

As Porrott watched him go, I told him what we had learnt
from him during the morning, none of which seemed to be
a great matter of astonishment to him; and indeed; we had
both seen the monkish garb upon Frederick. He picked up
the pistol and put it in his belt. It was not until I saw him
saddling Frederick's own great black steed that I realised
he meant to go after him. I clung on to him, crying that
Frederick might well have another pistol, and he could not
hope to overtake him after such a long time, even if he
could follow his track in the darkness.

"I know where he has gone. He and his friends have
a hide-out in a cave among the rocks at Brimham. And
the edges of the roads are muddy; I can soon see by the
moonlight if I am on the right track."

Again I begged him to stay behind, and asked what
business of us "thinking apes" it all was, but he put me
aside firmly and said, "It is because I am a man and not a
thinking ape – and you have taught me that" – and more
which I do not see fit to set down, but I shall never forget,
be it sixty years. Then he gave me the key to the monk's

box, with instructions to take it to Lord Fenborough and tell him everything if he had not returned by nightfall the next day.

He promised to wait at the door until I re-entered the house, and told me to go immediately to my chamber and put a candle in the window so he would know I was safe. This I did; and with what trouble did I see him raise his arm and wheel away into the darkness. The light is still burning and shall do so until he returns.

Then I composed myself, and let my mistress know I had returned by pretending I had heard her ring for me. I was not surprised when she joined me less than half an hour later. I wondered whether to tell her anything of what was afoot, but in my agitation I told her almost everything. " Poor Letty! This will kill her!" she cried out. I doubt it: one does not die for the asking. She said little more, but when she was in bed, drew me to her, and whispered, "Don't be afraid Celestine dear, he will come back. I know he will. " Dear child – I only wish I were so sure.

There was less moon than there had been on the night ride from Harrowgate and a brisk wind blew ragged patches of cloud across its face. But there was no frost to make the going treacherous and Porrot's eyes soon accustomed themselves to the dim light. From time to time he saw the unmistakeable marks of the muffled hooves in the mud, and he rode hard along the turnpike towards Brimham. He was a good while behind Frederick, but he had the advantage in that he and his mount knew one another, and he had the full use of both arms, for it was clear Frederick could only use his left arm with great difficulty. It was quite possible he might be thrown, especially when the track must be left behind and the horse pick its way through heather and whinberries.

He knew exactly where he was making for, a little cave near the base of a group of grotesquely shaped rocks leaning together. He had once been sent there to deposit a bundle, and had been met by two masked young men, who had taken it from him without a word. Porrott wondered what might be waiting there for Frederick – friends, a change of clothing, even a passport in a false name. One who has lived as dangerously as Frederick should provide himself with an escape route. He must not reach his sanctuary. Maybe it would be more rational to wait for the morrow and swear to his story before an attorney; but for all that he was going to stop him. Man to man he would conquer his master, and bring him back captive with evidence that none could gainsay. He had no wish to use his pistol, but he would defend his life, which had suddenly become worth the saving.

Was that a horseman ahead? Strange, he would not expect to be catching him yet, and the bags must have fallen from the hooves for he could hear their drumming far in front of him. There he was – far ahead – and as he drew closer he could see the rider bent low over his horse's neck urging it on. No, wait - that white patch on the rear hind leg – that's not Frederick; it's William. No problem to catch the little mare. He pushed his horse alongside, ready to grasp the bridle and force the truth from this double-dealing young man. As he came alongside William began to draw rein.

Both slowed to a walk, and William turned to Porrott with relief.

"Ah, how glad I am it is yourself: I had many fears. I suppose you are surprised to see me on this road? However it may seem, I am not an accomplice of his. I set out, indeed the other way, towards my friends at Harrowgate, but as the night air cleared my head it seemed to me a shameful thing to leave thus. A man offers to shoot me and I run from him like a rabbit! So I bethought me where he might take himself. I see you have the same knowledge. Have you a pistol? Nay, do not give it to me for I am a poor hand with a gun."

They kept company for a while, but the little mare's pace was slow and they decided that Porrott should press on while William made the best speed he could. Porrott surged forward; he longed to deal with his quarry himself.

Soon he had to leave the road. Progress was frustratingly slow, but possible, for the beast had picked his way over this country before. Suddenly the sky to the right and ahead was blotted out, and he knew he had come unawares among the great stone pillars. Below him, beside the stream, a bright spark showed where the gypsies had their fire. This told him where he was, and he set out towards the cave. Not far to his left he heard the scrape of iron on stone, and a muttered curse. Porrott moved his horse well in under the shadow of the rock as the moon came out again. Yes, Frederick was still in the saddle, though his whole body sagged as one deadly tired. His horse was lost, and stumbling among the higher rocks. Porrott watched and waited.

He was not the only watcher. The old gypsy woman nudged her grandson and pointed upwards from the fire.

" See him up there. Like Lucifer the Prince of Darkness in his pride. Aye; and in his evil."

"Why, grandmother, can you recognise a man from so far away? Who is he, and why does he deserve your blame?"

The old woman took her pipe from her mouth and spat in the fire. "Your father died when you were but five years old, and I never yet told you his story. Now is the time. When the young nobleman you see now on his charger was but a lad of seven or eight years old he used to wander the fields and woods near his home; aye, and this area too. For the lad was spirited though high-born, and liked nothing better than to give his tutors the slip and run wild, following his own devices. One cursed day he fell in with your father, but a young man himself, and they took a fancy to one another. From time to time they met by accident, and my son taught him a deal of animal lore, and showed him how to trap all beasts. Many times they went out together after hare and pheasant. I was uneasy, for oil and water do not mix, and I begged him to be careful, particularly when he had a wife and young son. But he would have it that the lad was his friend with a good love of sport, and called me a silly old woman. Well, one day they had a trifling disagreement – such as friends do from time to time – and the very next day my lad was taken up by the justices for poaching, and brought before Lord Fenborough himself, And it was that young man, whom he had loved as his own soul, that laid information against him. He was hanged at the next assizes. Now do you wonder that I know the man ? " She gazed into the depths of the fire and did not seem to notice when the boy stood up took a flaming brand from the fire and slipped away

But Porrott saw. Frederick had reined in his horse and sat motionless in the moonlight; the moonlight which showed him he was but a yard from the edge of a rocky mass, which plunged down before him and at the sides fifty feet to the darkness below. And as the groom watched, he saw a flaming arc fly up from the darkness and pass close before the eyes of the terrified horse. He saw the animal rear and leap forward, and was picking his way towards the dark lump on the ground before the noises had died away.

But of the firebrand he never spoke, considering that God may make use of strange instruments to bring about his justice.

Man and beast were killed outright. When William found them, the two men changed horses and William rode back to Skells to fetch the help that was needed. For the rest of the night Porrott remained beside the bodies, pondering on the terrible events, and resolving what he should say to his Lordship on the morrow. And by the time the party from the house arrived in the drizzling dawn, he knew what he must say to him.

Tuesday October 26th

He is safe! About an hour ago around three o'clock I heard hooves stop in the courtyard. I heard a hammering on the door, and cries and exclamations from within. Then I was out of the chamber – pausing only to lock the door behind me – and tearing down the staircase and along the passage to the kitchen.

There was confused bustling in the darkness and candles leapt to life. I could see he was not there, then heard the cook cry out, "What? Both dead?" and the sombre reply: " Aye in an instant." Then the table I was leaning against swayed like the deck of a ship and the candles buzzed round my head. A strong woman's arm sat me down, and held me awake. I heard again

"Both dead?"

And the reply;

"Aye, man and horse. The beast fell with his rider from a great height.".

I steadied myself to look across the table at the speaker. How could Mr Charlton be there? He swayed as he stood and his voice trembled. His face was pale beneath the bloodied bandage. But he went on, "We must get back there to bring him in. I left the groom standing guard. No, there is no time now to explain. One of you run and rouse his Lordship. Tell him" – and his face twisted a little – "tell him an urgent matter has arisen which the magistrate must see to immediately." He looked across at me, "What do you think, my girl? Should I take time now to speak with the ladies or leave them a few hours' happy ignorance?"

I urged him to go back at once, for the matter was urgent, and sat stupefied amid the bustle. I doubted he knew who I was, but I was wrong, for as he rose to set out he leaned forward and said to me very quietly, "He is unhurt."

To think I ever doubted that young man's heart and courage! They cannot be back for some hours. I will leave the candle alight and take what rest I can, for indeed I am very weary and troubled by what the day will bring upon us. But he is unhurt.

Celestine dreamed - In the moonlight the monk was chasing Araminta round and round among the pillars of the ruined church. His grey figure was everywhere – in front lying in wait, behind and gaining fast, poised above her on an archway – and her own feet were stuck fast in a gorse bush and all around were the moon and the pillars, with the monk still dodging, chasing and grinning. She begged Jacko, now grown tall as a man, to pull her out, but he leered and chattered at her and whisked his tail while the jewels in his ears sparkled in mockery. He leapt away to join in the chase, and Araminta turned and saw the horror approaching as the great wheels turned in her path – Celestine struggled awake, still to hear those wheels in the yard below.

The cart with its sad burden stopped and the riders reined in. Porrott was bone weary but he looked up and saw the candle flame wan in the daylight. The door swung open and household servants ran out, none of them looking directly at the cart or its load. They kept their distance and fell quiet, none sure what to say or do. As Porrott led his mare away he was aware of Celestine beside him. She took him through to the place where they had burned the letters, put the food and ale she was carrying on the table and lit the fire. He saw it all as through thick glass, eating without awareness and gradually, gently sensing the warmth. From a great distance he heard himself struggle to explain what had befallen, but he was stayed by her touch.

"Sleep first and talk later. Thank God you are safe!"

There was so much he should tell her, that she must know. So much too he must say to his Lordship that would not bear keeping, but his head was swimming and he discovered without astonishment that he was lying on his pallet and she had covered him with a cloak. And as she turned at the door and smiled he fought the tiredness no more, and slept.

The kitchen was full of lament. Most were weeping for shock, some for pity, some for companionship and a sense of what was fitting. The little pages crawled under the table and howled for fear in this strange world of weeping adults and clung to the monkey as it, trembling, clutched them. As Celestine left them and made her way back upstairs to her mistress a loud cry from the main apartments told her that Lord Fenborough was now with his wife and daughter. She hurried to reach Araminta with the news that no gentleness of manner could soften.

By mid-afternoon the ladies were in the drawing room. Lady Fenborough lay swooning on the sofa, her mother was upright beside her, holding her hand. Lady Hastings would not give way to sorrow in public but her shoulders sagged and there was hesitancy in her movements. Araminta was in the window-seat, holding Letty who sat on the floor with her head buried in her friend's lap. He shrieks had given way to ugly sobbing. Araminta placed a timid hand on her hair and leant over her, unconscious of her own persistent tears. Celestine sat quietly on an upright chair, loath to leave her young lady in this company of grief, but aware of a shameful impatience to know exactly what had happened and what it meant. She was guiltily irritated by the spectacle before her – such crying and lamenting for such a wicked, wicked man! She looked across at Lady Fenborough and wondered if the maid's story had had any truth in it. Lady Hastings roused her from her thoughts.

"Girl, go and find Leonie and tell her that her mistress needs her. Bid her dry her own tears and take up her common sense again. Then see if the physician is still in the house, and if he is send him here to tend my daughter."

When Celestine returned to the entrance hall after giving her messages she heard the bell at the front door. No other servant was in sight, so she opened to find the rector on the step. His mien was suitably grave, but Celestine thought she detected a hint of complacency as he stepped firmly inside, of pleasure that his calling made it proper and indeed necessary for him to arrive uninvited upon such a noble threshold at a time of crisis. She announced his arrival to the ladies. Lady Hastings rose to welcome him and dispatched her to the study, to inform his Lordship of the rector's arrival, "since you seem to be one of the few domestics not in a state of hysteria, intoxication or nervous prostration". The rector's calm professionally caring voice faded as she close the door behind her.

She had never before entered the study and she paused for a moment outside, reluctant to intrude upon his Lordship's grief. After a deep breath she opened the door and went in.

The first thing she saw was the monk's cloak, stained with blood, lying over the back of a chair that stood before the desk. Lord Fenborough was seated at the desk, elbows on the arms of his chair and hands clasped before him, staring ahead - not at the robe, but at the figure beside it - Porrott. Both men turned to look at her as she came in with her message.

"Ask him if he will be so good as to sit with the ladies for a while."

As she turned to go, she heard Porrott's voice. "My Lord, this is an opportune intrusion. It would be advisable to allow this young woman to remain, for she has information you should hear if we are to come to the truth of these dark matters.

Lord Fenborough looked at him in weary astonishment. But in a world so far upside down, why should not his servant speak thus? And there before them all was the dreadful evidence of the bloody cloak. He was, for the moment, incapable of setting his will against the other. In a voice without expression he said "Stay, then."

Silence in the room, apart from the strangely cheerful crackling of logs in the grate. At last he went on.

"You tell me you took this garment from my son's body before the rescue party arrived and put upon him the cloak you found in his saddle bag. Why?"

"My Lord, I am hardly sure, But it seemed to me more fitting that the whole household should not know of the monk's identity. Yet we are not alone in our knowledge: last night both this young woman and my young master's friend saw him enter the stables thus clad, and armed with a pistol." He explained what had taken place, calling on Celestine to supply what he had not himself witnessed.

"And that, then, is how there came to be a witness to his end? I would know – did he fall by accident from that place, or did he perhaps himself –"

"I am convinced he had no thought of self-destruction. The horse reared and slipped, while the master struggled to keep its balance."

"And you, girl. What were you about in the stables at that hour? A fine place for a young lady's attendant to be, alone and in the night!"

"Unhappily, but clearly, she gave the gist of what she had learned from Mr Charlton, and why she had been there. Lord Fenborough lowered his head and stared at the desk top. Again a long silence.

"And what more have you to tell me?" Both servants could see he was troubled, but neither incredulous nor indignant

Celestine thought that beneath his calm manner he was hurriedly preparing a course of action. When his eyes flicked upwards for a moment she saw they were as watchful as a swordsman's.

"A great deal, sir, and little enough of it welcome. Your young lady guest walking in her sleep suddenly woke and saw the monk abroad on the night the druid met his death. Later I took this box from the place where Celestine, on a later occasion, saw him conceal it. If you will examine it carefully, your Lordship," and he put the box on the polished desk top, "you will see green moss caught in the corner of the lid. No such moss grows where the box was found, but it grows in abundance in the druid's cell. There is a niche lined with this moss, hidden by trailing ivy, near where the druid had his bed. This moss has a jagged tear in it, as if some sharp object has been dragged along it. I am sure the monk took the box from there, and also that he could not have done so during the druid's lifetime."

"Why so?"

"Celestine, the key." She loosed it from where she had pinned it inside her pocket and handed it to him. He swung up the lid, and took out the little notebook which he passed across the desk. "I believe this was too valuable and too dangerous to the druid to be in any hands other than his own. This will make clear the nature of his treasure." Lord Fenborough turned over the pages of the little book. "There were also some half dozen letters, all addressed to different people. These we have burned, unread."

"Did you recall to whom they were sent?"

"No sir, I do not. Neither of us can recall any of the names." This with a warning glance to Celestine. "But it is all too clear what sort of a fellow the druid was, and how he got fat by extortion. There were other items in the box, which I put in a bag and replaced where the box had been found."

"Why?"

"They were of too great a value to risk their discovery among my effects. You may wish to see this inventory." He handed across a list.

"£200 in gold… three purses… diamond necklace, pearl earrings, pearl and diamond earrings, sapphire brooch and bracelet… What is all this?"

"Sir, I believe the money in the main to be the product of the druid's extortions, and as for the rest, it looks like the hoard of a robber. Indeed, I believe it to be so, for I have heard of the jewels taken by highway robbery from a coach on the moors within the last month, and in particular of a lady who lost her sapphire brooch and bracelet."

"So you suspect the druid of this ?"

"I do not say so, my Lord. As I see it, this box suggests either that the druid and the monk were conspirators (particularly when we remember the story that Mr Charlton told) or that the monk for some reason slew the druid and stole the box, adding to it items of his own."

"But why should he wish to - "

"Perhaps they were conferates who quarrelled over some item of property; perhaps the druid tried his extortioner's tricks on the monk. I do not know, having no evidence. But I have evidence that the druid was not killed in the Temple of Piety by yew berries but in his own cell. There are clear marks on the trees where the body was dragged through the wood. I also know that the wrists of your son were covered in scratches when I saw them this morning and believe they were made on Friday night when a foolish maid recognised the monk and boasted to him of it. It is true she was not found until the next morning, but I have not found anyone who saw her after that evening.

The fire was burning low unheeded and the light began to fade from the window.

Lord Fenborough cleared his throat. His hands were at his temples, but he fixed Porrott with a firm gaze.

"So you are accusing my son of the druid's death?"

"All the facts I have given you will indeed support that interpretation. But I can imagine another one. Just suppose... this story would begin far in the past, say twenty years ago"

"So long?"

"So long. Suppose a young married lady, who in secret bears a son by one that is not her lawful spouse. Suppose she presents him to her husband as his own. She, or someone else, perhaps her mother, dismisses the servant who acted as midwife. She believes herself safe. The child thrives and is accepted by all as his father's heir. Who knows how her heart and conscience misgive her? But then she discovers herself prey to a man – one of her husband's employees, perhaps, who knows her secret. For years he torments her; he is one whose delight is in causing pain and watching its effects. In the end she becomes resigned to his demands, for Time accustoms his patients to long suffering, but then a crisis approaches. Her son will soon come of age;

her tormentor pretends to a conscience and swears he will make public his knowledge. She goes by night to plead with him – perhaps more than once – and finally she finds him in a drunken sleep. In a moment snatches up a cover and stifles him, then she searches wildly for the written proof she believes him to have, without success, for it never existed. Then."

"Surely you forget that the body was found in the Temple of Piety? It would be a strong lady who could carry him there, far stronger than…"

"I had not finished, my Lord. Suppose her to return to her chamber distracted and overwhelmed with horror. There she wakes her husband, and gasps out her story to him. Whatever his own feelings he is willing to help her. Then suppose him to drag the body to another place, losing threads from his coat and wig as he makes his way through the undergrowth with his burden. He arranges it so as to suggest the man made away with himself by means of poison. In his anxiety to protect his wife he returns to the cave to discover if anything has been overlooked. It is dark and he is very troubled. Small wonder if he overlooks the box – and this."

Porrott opened his hand and showed a single emerald and diamond earring. "This was found in the box. At first I thought of it as part of the robber's hoard, but where was its pair? Then I heard from Celestine her mistress's account of the coach ride from Harrowgate. Celestine, could this be the match of the earring that the monkey snatched from her ladyship's bag?"

Celestine looked carefully; I think it could be. My mistress told me it was a cluster of three emeralds with a diamond drop beneath." Porrott looked at his Lordship as if awaiting a reply. After a silence, he continued. "I believe the monk, once he found the druid was dead, ransacked the cell for the lucrative letters, found this on the ground and recognised it."

"But surely, "Celestine broke in, "would not any man have quietly returned it – his own mother!"

"Most men would, indeed. But this one saw how it might one day profit him, and he kept it with his other instruments of extortion."

"Why have you told me this? What do you expect of me? Have you spoken to any other?"

"My Lord, a sealed letter has been lodged with an attorney to be opened only on my death or at my express command."

"And will you give that command? Your story may be plausible but it is lacking in some details. Suppose this lady of your imagination to have been long suffering from a wasting disease of flesh as well as spirit, and suppose her physicians to have said that within a few weeks she will be subject to no human justice. Suppose too that she has a daughter who is as innocent of all this as the dawn itself, a girl who has lost a beloved brother and whose mother is soon to die: need she lose more and know what darkness has underlain her whole life? Need she be utterly disgraced?"

Celestine spoke quietly with Porrott, while his Lordship sat motionless, staring into the fire. Porrott nodded, and turned back to Lord Fenborough. He spoke quietly.

"Celestine has seen some of what you tell me in her Ladyship's face, and it weighs with me far more than a foolish girl's delusions. But something else weighs with me even more; the husband's forbearance towards three strangers who innocently came upon the Temple while the corpse was being displayed. For though I believe he saw them, and was never sure that they did not know enough to destroy him, and though two of them were but servants, he did them no harm. Sir, it is mainly for your forbearance to the lady who I hope will become my wife that I will leave the letter sealed. I am no great student of the Scriptures, but I call to mind a verse, 'Blessed are the merciful, for they shall obtain mercy,'"

The fire had almost died by now, and the room was darkening. His Lordship's face could not be seen, After a while he spoke; "I am greatly obliged – indeed, I thank you. I do wonder, my girl," to Celestine, "if your young lady's father would agree to take my daughter home with him for a while, for the next few weeks here will be sad and weary. And I insist – no, I beseech you – that she shall never hear this story. Not even when – as must sooner or later befall – she becomes an orphan. You will not find me ungrateful."

"Being neither monk nor druid, I have no need of a bribe, sir. My employment here with your son is now at an end. I wish only for the wages that are due to me. I will go north tomorrow with the others who leave."

They left him alone in the dark room.

Friday October 29th

Dear, dear Louisa,

How sorry you will be when you read this, after waiting all day for us only to see a lone horseman with news and letters. But alas we are marooned by the weather in this farmhouse. How I hope it will only be for one more day.

Take good note of the messenger. You will remember how merry we all were the night before we went away and how you teased me and bade Celestine take care I came back to you heart whole? So do I, whether or not thanks to Celestine's care, but I fear you were apprehensive for the wrong person! Yes, this horseman, who is Porrott of whom I have made mention has had the audacity and good fortune to win the heart of our Celestine, and within a few months he is likely to take her away from us, though she has promised to remain until the Spring, so that he can cast about for some suitable employment and she can initiate Lizzie into the arts and skills she needs to be a lady's maid. I shall miss her indeed, but not enough to wish her never to have her own home and husband. Alas, I have learned of late that nothing can be relied on to remain the same. When I look back on that night in the kitchen, I feel I left home a child and return a woman.

My dear, I will not try to describe to you the two days after poor Frederick's body was brought home. I could not write nor you read without tears. With what joy and relief I heard the coach draw up in the courtyard and raced out to fall upon my dear parent's breast, your own heart will tell you! I clung to him with an indescribable sense of safety and was again the little girl he lifted to his shoulder when she was frightened by the lowing of the cows.

I was astonished to discover that Letty was to travel with us and be our guest for a while (to you, and you alone, I will confess a selfish wish that she should not do so) but I learnt from Celestine that her father wishes her to be away from home because her mother is very ill indeed. Later I said to Papa that I hoped he would not try to send me away if our mother was in like case, for I would not go, and I wondered how Lord Fenborough could be so cruel as to dismiss his daughter at such a time. But Father told me I must not consider Lord Fenborough unkind: "From what he has said to me, my dear, no-one could have a more tender care for his daughter than has Letty's father." Then he clasped me to him. And added, "Families and daughters differ, Minta, I could not send you away."

Well, we were all eager to be off, and we left on the same afternoon. Father, Letty. Her little dog Laura, her maid, Celestine and I in the coach, James and Edwin on the box, and Porrott riding with us on a horse Lord Fenborough had given him. He was to be useful to us on our journey and the perhaps stay in our service for a short time. Lady Fenborough did not appear to say farewell, and I am glad of it. I have never found her comfortable to speak with and now, knowing how sick and sorrowful she is, I would have been hard put to speak as I should. His Lordship appeared to put Letty in the coach. He was very stiff and formal and I faltered out my farewells without daring to look directly at him. As the vehicle rolled over the cobbles the last I saw was the cook comforting the little black pages who were howling lustily; I suppose for the loss of their friend from the stables.

With what different emotions did I pass out through the gates of the estate than I entered them less than three weeks ago! I sat gazing from the window in silence as we rattled over the wet highway.

We stopped at an inn in Pateley Bridge to feed and water the horses. As Celestine and I crossed the in yard a country girl in a blue dress came rushing up. She curtseyed to us and spoke excitedly to Celestine, and I realised from what she said that she must be the niece of the woman at the turnpike cottage. It is no wonder she spoke to Celestine with such respect and affection. Celestine asked her about the family's welfare and the girl – Betty is her name, and she used to be a servant at Skells – took her by the hand.

"Oh yes, yes, thanks to you miss. The little girl is quite happy now, and I often hear her telling the doll the story she says you told her, and the baby is thriving, and my poor uncle is not nearly so bad as we thought he would be at first. And something else, the strangest thing! I can tell you now, for he can trouble us no longer. You will never guess who it was that was behind the mob that attacked the cottage – he roused them up and came with a friend of his on horseback and watched and waited in the shadows it seems. It was that-"

Celestine interrupted her. "Do not speak so loud Betty. You will waken poor Miss Laetitia and her maid who are resting in the coach exhausted by their grief and" – in a lower voice – "ignorant of much that we know."

"Well, " went on Betty, much more quietly, "I hope I may tell you for everybody in the valley knows it bar the constable and the justices. You remember the great coach robbery about a month ago on the moors? No, of course you will not, for it was before you came here, but there was one, and a masked man with a pistol held up a coach and carried off I don't know how much money and jewels. It seems my uncle saw the highwayman as his horse leapt the turnpike gate, and he recognised him by the way he rode his horse – and it seems he was afraid he might have recognised him and be inclined to reveal what he knew and so he came to the cottage with a mob to make sure he would never dare to speak out for fear of something worse. And though it seems a cruel thing to say – and indeed the Good Book says we should not rejoice at the death of a sinner – I am sure this valley will be a cleaner and happier place for two of the violent deaths we have seen. How I wish Sarah had come back with us that night! It was a wicked thing he did to her. Yet," glancing at the carriage, "I cannot but be sorry for miss Laetitia and her parents. But goodbye, my dear Celestine, and you too ma'am, God keep you and I am sorry you will carry away such ill memories of this place."

Celestine kissed her farewell and we saw her run back across the yard to join a burly young man driving a cart, and I knew her for the same girl who had ridden away in tears on that very cart the day we were watching for Porrott to return with news of the druid's death. The young man was the same too. No tears now in the eager look she gave him.

That night, while Celestine was helping Letty's maid to tend her in her room, Father and I sat and talked before the fire. I told him of all my terrors and adventures, and wept as I had not dared before. Perhaps by the time I am home I will be able to make a lively tale of it all for the younger ones. I told him I was not clear what had happened, for though Celestine told me something of it during the past two days when we were in our room I had been too distraught and unhappy to understand fully what she had said. So he told me that it seemed Frederick in the guise of the monk, had been engaged in various wicked deeds, and was probably an associate of the druid's and had fallen out with him and killed him; not in the Temple of Piety where I came upon his body but in his cell. He told me that the druid had been a very wicked man, who made his living by most cruel extortion. So William was quite right in his estimation of Frederick. When I recall with what silly thoughts and hopes I cam here I shudder to think that I could ever have imagined – indeed, I am disgusted that I have danced with him. And how I admired his supposed courage that night, when his bravest action was to drown a kitchen maid like a kitten! All, all a sham. Dear sister, have a care to whom you give your heart! (Do I not sound edifying, and like a grandmother from one of the stories Aunt Jemima used to read to us?) For all that he was handsome, and much taller than William, who came to bid us farewell with great attention. He is a kindly man though, and I would be pleased to number him among my cousins.

We were making good time on Thursday, and at last we came over a hill and I looked across and there in the distance were our own blue fells against the horizon.. How I longed to leap from the lumbering coach, kilt up my skirts, and run all the way home to you. I was fit to burst with impatience as the coach crawled along the road, and worse was to come, for it grew suddenly cold, the wind cut keenly and snow began to fall, a few flakes at first but then a swirling blinding curtain.

We took refuge at the next farm we found where the good farmer's wife brought us blankets and hot broth which we sorely needed. Alas the snow continued all night, and though it had stopped by morning Papa decided it was not safe to go on in the carriage. I begged to continue, pleading that if aught did go amiss we could always walk to the next farm and hire ourselves some horses, but he gravely reminded us that Letty was with us. "I know you and Celestine can walk many a mile in snow if needs be, Minta, but what of your poor friend? She is already sick with grief, and it would be the death of her. No, my dear, you must cheer up and show your courage. You are safe with me, and 'twill be but a day or two."

And I hope so. I must finish in a minute for Porrott is almost ready to depart and he must take this letter with him.

And so I close the final letter of this strange journey of mine, glad to have left the splendid buildings and grounds where cruelty and death lurked and stalked unchecked, and longing for our own dear home. I can see you all running out to meet us, Nellie with flour to her elbows, mother shading her eyes against the sunset, you holding back Shep and the little ones tumbling to the gate, while on the hill behind our own great oak stands sentinel, to bless and protect us all.

And I shall be with you soon!

All my love,
Araminta

CPSIA information can be obtained
at www.ICGtesting.com
Printed in the USA
LVOW03s0125130318
569660LV00001B/29/P